Gabriel

Olivia Burge

Contents

Chapter ~ 1

S ocial hierarchy || Gabriel Lewis

Freezing. Teeth chattering, shivering, chilled to the bone, freezing. Call me Elsa cause I'm damn well near being frozen.

It's no miracle really, the square framed hole, lined with shards of glass in my wall, let's in the icy winter winds in my room, the cut up blanket that was stuck over the former window with duct tape, the thin material only did so much in keeping the cold air outside. Not to mention the multiple holes and cracks in the ceiling, it's no mystery on why my small room is turning into what I imagine the back of Narnia's wardrobe to be, minus the clothing.

My door creaked loudly as it was opened, feet shuffling on the old timber flooring, my eyes cracked open, seeing the small blurred out line of my two younger siblings, hands no doubt intertwined tightly while their other hands held on to their comfort items.

A dirty dark grey stuffed cat, named scatcat, clutched tightly to Jack's chest, his super man pyjama pants pooling around his feet, being slightly too long for him, an old faded buzz light year singlet covering his chest.

His twin, Lillian, held on to a dirty red cotton blanket, that has been dragged behind her ever since she could crawl, her fingers gripping the edge, her thumb between her teeth, leaving permanent intents in her skin, a bad habit she has yet to break out of.

"Gabe?" A soft voice mumbled, slicing through the night air, my arm was already lifting blankets up, I shuffled my body backwards until my back hit the wall, allowing the two small children to climb into my bed. Lillian pressed her small body against my chest, Jack climbing in afterwards, his small arms wrapping around his sisters waist, she placed the small blanket over them before i covered them with my blanket. My arm wrapping around them both.

This was more or less a nightly routine in the cooler months, their body's ending up curled into my chest, the combined body heat of the three of us, keeping up from being completely frozen, them more so then me.

My rundown home wasn't anything to be proud of, the walls were paper thin, the electrics were shadier then the dark side of the moon and it was quiet frankly falling apart, which seemed to be the ongoing theme for the houses in my broke neighbourhood. No mater the state it's in or location, it's a roof over my head which my father works hard to keep. Working multiple jobs, to keep us from going into debt and keeping my mother alive.

A 30 minute walk in the middle of winter wasn't something that I particularly enjoyed, due to the fact I'm as active as a sloth on steroids. Both of my hands were taken up by my siblings, their small gloved hands gripping mine as they walked beside me, naming the colours of the cars that sped past, as we made our way to school.

Jack and Lilian's primary (elementary) school was a ten minute walk past my own, dropping them off at their class, My hand running through Jacks soft blond locks a few time to fix his hair, while Lillian's arms were wrapped tightly around my neck, "have a good day" I mumbled to the both of them, pulling jack in to my side to include him in the hug. Pressing a kiss to the side of his head, before prying his twin sister's arms from my neck.

"I love you both. I'll see you after school alright?" I told them softly, pulling gently at Lillian's wrist to stop her from sucking on her thumb. Bidding good bye I made my way out of the school grounds, heading towards hell's dungeon or my school.

Once I arrived, more or less, undetected and unscathed apart from a few degrading names and the usual glares shot my way. Though my cheep luck was short lived as my usual up close and personal meeting with the concrete floors commenced. My glasses sliding from my head and dropping to the floor, my fingers patted the area under my head, picking my glasses up and putting them on once again.

The smirking face of James Hiller looking down at me, his friends snickering beside him. Sighing, I picked my self up to my knees, dusting the dirt off my forarms. "Sup queer"James sneered, one of his friends, picking me up roughly, my lips are sealed as I look at him with a bored expression. I had almost no sleep the past few nights and couldn't care less for what James has up his sleeve, maybe if he punched me hard enough I'll go unconscious and actually be able to sleep.

Unfortunately the punch never came, they just pushed me around like a rag doll, my legs getting tangled a few times causing me to stumble which seems to be comedy gold for the uneducated swines that surround me.

I almost laugh at the mention of my school, honestly it was the most judgemental and stereotypical American school in all of North Dakota if not all of America. Your cliché groups of people, all marked on the invisible popularity chart or food chain of the school.

The 'bad boy' or boy with a criminal history who isn't afraid to show off why; would be first, purely from everyone else either being fearful of him or wanting to get into his pants, then you have Football Jocks and the respective cheerleading team, all at the very top of the popularity food chain. The basketball and swim team fighting for the 3rd place and any cheerleader that is good enough in bed to be in a relationship with them.

Me? I'm at the bottom of the food chain, the very dark, cold, lonely bottom, that no one goes or wants to gets them self stuck there with the amount of shit that drops from the people above. I've gotten use to it over the years, and it doesn't bother me as much as it probably should with all the bullying. I rather it be me with my pathetic life then some other kid that has dreams and aspersions that actually could come true.

"You alright Gabe?" A kind and familiar voice asked, a hand gripping my arm softly, large, wide brown eyes glancing up at me with concern. Claire Holland, an under appreciated cheerleader for the basketball team, with her petite body and kind heart, she the personality exception to the rule of stereotypical cheerleaders.

"Fucking Assholes the lot of them" she muttered glaring at the backs of the jocks that were walking away. "I'm fine" I replied, the lie slipping through my teeth easily, my lips joined in on the lie by curving into a fake smile, just to sell the act of being okay. She didn't look convinced, her calculating eyes studying my face before shaking her head.

"You look terrible" she muttered, unconvinced of my Emmy award winning performance of being okay. I huff out a laugh readjusting the straps on my backpack. "Your compliments are the confidence boosters i live for" I muttered sarcastically, rolling my eyes. Scoffing she slapped my arm playfully, bidding good byes as she walked to her awaiting friends.

Stopping at my locker to get the items I require, I made my way to class. Ignoring the taunts and snickers from my cell mates in this hell. Arriving I did my magic disappearing act, hiding my head in my arms, for my own sanity and peace of mind, I told my self if I can't see them, they can't see me.

"Wake up dike" a voice came before my head was lifted harshly by my hair, I winced glancing up at the face, he smirked grabbing my glasses, I already knew the fate of the glasses as he dropped them to the floor and smashed them under his foot. The pack of hyenas crackled at their own antics before leaving me be and the hair on my head mostly intact.

My vision was blurred, the once sharp lines of words became fuzzy and unreadable, along with everything and everyone else. Granted the glasses were 'cheep' knock offs from local chemist that sells non prescription glasses between the sunglasses and sunscreen, but the $25 price tag adds up quickly as my glasses are snapped on a regular basis.

"Today you'll be getting an assignment, though slightly different then then the usual. Over the years of teaching in this school it has accrued to me that our school -and schools with in America- are vastly different to those around the world." Miss Justine said, pacing slowly across the classroom.

"My cousin lives in a city called Perth, which is in Western Australia. Her daughter goes to secondary school just like you lot but the dynamics and relationships between class mates and other school peers are very different." She explained walking to her desk and handing out sheets of paper.

"Popularity isn't a huge deal, yes bullying still goes on but unlike here, no one is put into a group or a social hierarchy, they all are on an equal playing ground. The high achievers are awarded and praised for their achievements, they are friends with the sporting groups. Unheard of I know." Miss Justine explained, i let out a chuckle, looking down at the assignment outline, not that I could read it.

"The assignment you have in front of you is to write, minimum of 2 pages, biography of someone who isn't in your social group. Learn who they are, you never know you might have more in common then you think. You are expected to visit your respective partners -which I have chosen- outside of school to complete this assignment" Miss Justine explained, earning a groan from the whole class at the idea of working with someone outside their social group.

Since any social interaction with me is considered social suicide, I already felt sorry for the poor soul that had to work with me. God help me if it's any of the Ku klux - I mean the football team as my partner.

"Jaxon, so nice for you to join us, please find your seat next to Gabriel, as he is your assignment partner"

Well paint me green and call me a pickle.

Chapter ~ 2

Time || Gabriel Lewis

Time goes by so slowly. It was almost to agonising to watch the clock, since it seemed to only go slower with my eyes concentrated on it. I just wanted the day to end, not that it's been a particularly bad day apart from the fact I now have a partnered English assignment with Jaxon Coles, the king on top of the hill with his shoe kissing servants below him, sucking up to him anyway they could to get a second glance.

My eyes glanced lowly around the rest of the class, they all were chatting happily with each other. Since the class task required you to work in a small groups, but considering I have no friends nor any volunteers that want be seen with me, I had to work on it by my self which I didn't mind as I've completed it, everyone else not so much.

"Wednesday. Four pm, your house" a low voice grumbled, startling me slightly, glancing up Jaxon's figure was already walking out of the classroom before I could say a word. Firstly Wednesday i can't do nor will it he be anywhere near my house. I have a list of things that I get bullied for, my living conditions is not something I want to add to the list. The bell rang loudly, my body was already up and running out of the room to catch up with Jaxon.

"Jaxon!" For some stupid reason I decided to shout his name with in hearing range of everyone, so in other words I just signed my death wish. The halls went quiet, making me cringe. They all looked at me as if I had lost my mind, which I'm highly considering it to be a possibility.

He turned to look at me, raising an eyebrow, the simple words that I was going to say slipped out of my mind. My eyes glancing nervously at the large crowd that is burning holes in my body with their stares. A sudden force of somebody pushing me forwards had me falling face first. Landing on my arms, which sent shots of pain up my arms with the landing.

"What would the pathetic little fag like you, have to say to, well, anyone really?" James sneered, his foot coming in contact with my side, I hissed in pain, trying to get up. I swear I hate everyone here, they all just watch like good for nothing sheep in a heard. Grumbling, I stood up wincing at the pain in my side where James so kindly kicked it.

"I can't do Wednesday and definitely not my house" I spat out before walking off, anger Bubbled inside of my stomach, I seem to be the only one suffering in that whole school. I never see anyone get bullied apart from me. I was the schools punching bag, and for what? Cause I'm gay? Honestly the lot of them make me sick.

"Gabe!" A female voice called out, hurried footsteps behind me before an hand grabbed my arm. "Gabe" Claire huffed out, halting my movements. "Are you okay? I saw what happened" she asked out concern filling her blurry features. I shook my head, before forcing out a laugh.

"Why do you care?" I asked my voice coming out harshly, not that I really cared at the moment. She looked taken back at my tone, catching her breath, before answering. "Because I like you, your my friend" she stated, shock and surprise filtered through my system but was quickly burnt out by the small fire that burned in my stomach.

"Friend? Don't give me that bull crap Claire. If a friend is only going to talk to me or care when no ones looking then I'd rather be a loner" I muttered turning away from her and continued to walk, squinting my eyes in a futile attempt to get better eyesight.

I don't know what's gotten into me, I probably just ruined everything between the one person who treats me like I'm human not a sewer rat, but I'm not going crawling back because it's the truth. Are people really your friend if their reputation means more to them then you?

The large grins of my siblings, doused the flames with in, as all anger was forgotten, their bodies colliding with mine as they ran into my open arms. Their small arms wrapping around my neck and shoulders. "How are my favourite 5 year olds? Did you two have a good day?" I asked pressing a kiss to both of their foreheads, before standing, holding their small hands as we walked out of the school grounds.

They answered excitedly listing the events that happened in their day. Unlike myself, the twins love school, they rave about it and apart from the early rise and walk, they would go everyday if they could, to play with their friends and learn new things. I guess when everything was so simple school is fun, there is no real judgment at that age.

I've always wanted a friend, just someone who would be by my side, that I could talk and rant to. Someone who didn't care about my living conditions, understood my home situations with my mother. Just someone there for me, but that sadly is a unrealistic dream coming from my standpoint.

It's always been me against the world, with my mother sick and my father working multiple jobs to keep us from losing something, the twins being to young to understand anything, I really have no one. Let me tell you, it's gets pretty damn lonely.

"Evening mum" I greeted softly, walking into the semi-private hospital room. She smiled weakly in return, her eyes held no light to them anymore, her once golden locks have been replaced with a head scarf, her skin looked pale and sticky.

"How's school?" She asked, lies spewed from my mouth, all about my nonexistent friends and experiences that I could only dream of having but knowing it won't. I didnt tell her the truth cause she didn't need to hear all bad crap that my life was plagued with. She was sick and laying more of less in her death bed.

I wish I could get a job and help my father out with the bills, hell maybe have extra to spend, but with the twins being so young, they need someone there and I can't take care of them if I have a job.

The twins were to young to understand what's wrong with their mother, or why their father was never around, just me. I've basically raised them for the past two and a half years, Im the guy who they turn to for help, Im the one who leaves school early or takes days off when they fall ill. I've had to grow up and become their big brother and their parents all in one.

"Mummy! Look" Lillian said crawling up on my lap so she should reach mother easier, a piece of paper clutched in her hand. "For you! Me, Gab and jack going to school and you on top of the rainbow" she explained her scribbles and stick figures. I smiled pressing my lips to the top of her head, mother giving her a smile.

"Looks beautiful Sweetheart" mother commented softly, tears shining in her eyes. It broke my heart to see my mother the way she is, the sadness in her eyes kills me every time I look in them. I sometimes wonder if she really wants to be here. If she still wants to live or if she just holds on because of us? My fingers intertwined with my mother's, rubbing my thumb over the back oh her hand comfortingly.

The doctors found 4 tumours spread on her brain, three years ago, which were removed and all was fine, only to find six months later that cancer was attacking her lungs and other parts of her body, which had already spread to far to have any chance at successful treatment.

So mother was diagnosed with Terminal lung and bronchial cancer, after awhile home wasn't the best place for her so she was moved to the hospital where she can get 24/7 care. Doctors say she is a miracle that she has survived this long.

Monday's, Wednesday's and Friday's, I bring the twins over after school. Father can only make it on sundays which is his only day off which is divided between the twins and mother, though Mum is usually first choice. We only see my father for a few hours if that, on Sunday since he goes to bed very early to make up for lost time.

I pressed a kiss to my mother's forehead, whispering I love you to her before getting the twins ready for the journey home. We take a buss that stops at the shops near our home then walk the rest of the way.

The twins bid their goodbyes, Waving with their free hand as the other was holding me. I lead them through the hospital halls, greeting the familiar nurses on the way.

My mouth became dryer then the Sahara desert, Jaxon Coles standing -hardly- infront of me, he looked horrible with blood stains everywhere and a swollen eye. His eyebrow only raised slightly when he spotted me, his eyes drifting down to the children by my side.

"Did he get into a fight?" Jack asked failing majorly at art of whispering, though he did try, the question was still in hearing range of the beat up boy. "Yes, he fights little boys who don't listen to their big brother" I replied watching Jack's eyes widen comically, glancing at me nervously. I laughed shaking my head, earning a pout from Jacks as he figured out my small fib.

"Your mean" he whined trying to hold back a smile which ended up taking over his face. I grinned winking at him, giving a playful nudge with my arm.

"Tomorrow or Thursday's, your house or anywhere somewhat child friendly." I said standing beside him, I didn't get a respond from him, only a emotionless stare.

Time to go home.

Grace XOX

Chapter ~ 3

- -

U nexpected || Gabriel Lewis

Bad decisions, if it was an Olympic sport I'd win gold with no real competition. Like when I was seven, we had a cat called Garfield. I'm guessing rolling in dirt and mud must of been it's favourite past-time apart from sleeping for this overweight cat cause it always came home covered in dirt, and stunk too.

So being the smart and helpful child I was, I decided to give the cat a wash, one it will never forget. Let's just say, Garfield was traumatised, he never stepped foot in the bathroom again and had a irrational fear of flushing toilets. It was a childhood mystery on why that cat never liked me after that.

Today, my first bad decision, which started the avalanche horrible decisions was waking up. I know one would think the art of waking up could almost be impossible to stuff up but in my case I should of continued to sleep. Coming in close second place, would be going to school, that decision ultimately was me digging my own grave, School was a suicide mission.

I bit my bottom lip, holding in the groan of pain that so badly wanted to escape my mouth. I guess the school wasn't over my poor misjudgment of the consequences with talking to their royal high-ass. My arms were shielding my face, keeping them from smashing the second pair of my glasses this week. It was only Tuesday.

The two pairs of hands that were holding my arms tightly so I wouldn't run and holding my weight up against the lockers as James continues his assault of punches to my stomach. The heavenly sound of the bell, echoed loudly through the halls, saving me from anymore abuse this morning. The two apes holding me up let go, allowing me to collapse to the ground with as much grace as falling sack of potatoes.

Once last kick to the stomach, made the cry of pain escape, in response laughter. It hurt everywhere, standing at that moment was not an option since my torso screamed pain from the beating.

This was the worst it's ever been. I never got bashed up, I got name calling which is easy to ignore and some pushing around, a ball aimed for me in sports sometime but never a real beating like today.

The worst part of the whole thing is that no one cared. No one would notice my absence in class, or even help, they watch and walk away like nothing ever happened, if anyone asked, they all would shrug and carry on with life, not batting an eyelid if it doesn't concern them.

My parents wouldn't even know, they both have enough on their plate then to worry about me or the twins for that matter, that was my job. Mum counted her days in a hospital bed, Dad paid the bills and I take care of the twins, making sure they are as happy as can be so they don't end up like me. Depressed and lonely.

Managing to get my self sitting, leaning against the lockers. lifting my shirt, glancing down at my torso, cuts from the ring he was wearing littered my already red skin, no doubt becoming bruises. The kick from yesterday has become a nice bruise.

"The fuck happened to you?" A familiar voice snapped, straightening my glasses I looked up seeing Jaxon looking down at me, his face slightly cut up from what ever happened yesterday.

"What does it look like?" I grumble figuring my day wouldn't be getting any better and getting knocked out sounds like heaven right now. Getting up was a painful experience that had tears stinging my eyes. When hell freezes over will I cry in front of Jaxon Coles.

My body was still leaning heavily on the lockers behind me, I half wondered what Jaxon was still doing in front of me, it struck me that I might be in front of his locker. Cringing as I limped out of the way of the locker I was blocking.

I had my two options, try and survive the rest of the day in this hell hole or attempt the half an hour walk home, which makes this afternoon's trip double. Glancing out the glass doors, Mother Nature has so kindly chosen for me. I guess I'm staying.

Jaxon didn't move from his spot, standing their with his arms crossed making his biceps bulge more then usual, I didn't let my mind wonder to much further down that dangerous path. His eyes starting at me, with a mask of no emotion, which made him look pissed off. I really wanted to know what was running through his head right now cause I'd rather not be bashed up again, specially by him.

"Our project. Lunch today, cafeteria ." He said before walking off, i huffed rolling my eyes, yeah if I make it to lunch. Groaning I limped to my locker, chucking my bag into it roughly, before grabbing my books for class, which I was fifteen minutes late for.

I couldn't decide wether it took forever for lunch to come around or if it was to fast. Either way I was not looking forward to what's to come with in the next 40 minutes.

Why Jaxon wants to do the project at lunch and in the most crowed place is beyond me. If I got beaten for simply calling his name, I don't want to know what James and his pack of vultures, will have in store for me if I'm seen sitting with him at lunch.

I sighed, closing my locker door, dreading the next episode of WWE. Staring me, the unfortunate soul who will surely lose, the underdog that beats the stereotype and has no support.

Walking in to the cage of death also know as the school cafeteria, my eyes scanned the room looking for the boy I'm currently risking my life for. Because luck is never on my side and the world loves to see my pain, Jaxon was siting on the bench at the other end, meaning I had to pass the jocks and everyone else to reach him.

Considering I never set foot in the cafeteria because to enter you'd need to have friends, something I lack. I also rather be anywhere else then around the people who cause me pain.

I was hoping that no one would notice, since everyone has friends or food that would be much more interesting but apparently my unwanted presence is much more. Everything stoped, literally. I've made it five steps in and have the whole cafeteria looking at me with a mixture of emotions, none of which are good. A low murmur of confusion and my heart beating out of my chest in nervousness, was all I heard.

Forcing my feet to move, I continued. Is this what people feel like when they get court doing the walk of shame? I haven't done anything wrong yet I feel like a wanted criminal walking into a police station.

"Where the fuck do you think your going?" James' voice spat, standing in front of me, blocking my path. My response was silence as I kept my eyes on the floor, apparently it wasn't the correct answer. A punch to the gut, was enough to double me over in pain, i braced for the second.

Skin met skin with a harsh slap, a collective of gasps following straight after. I was confused cause James' first never reached me for the second punch. My jaw dropped when I straightened up, looking wide eyed at Jaxon, who had jame's fist in the palm of his hand, which was centimetres away from where my face was.

"Enough" Jaxon spat angrily, pushing the fist away, his body was angled in front of me, blocking me. My head was going haywire, trying to comprehend the events that are taking place.

Jaxon Coles stood up for me.

Not only that, it's in front of most of the school, I didn't know what to think. In the back of my mind I figured this is only cause of the project, and by tomorrow morning I will be dead meat, but in this moment, I couldn't care less. Someone who I'd never thought would be bothered to put the effort in standing up for me, stoped james in front of the school.

Jaxon grabbed my arm pushing me forward, past a dumbfounded gaping James, who has been trying to become buddy buddy with Jaxon for years, it's half the reason Jaxon has become untouchable and the king of the school.

Jaxon walked behind me as I neared the table, the familiar face of Hunter Gillies, the other half of the dynamic duo and best friend of Jaxon. He had a bit more of a friendly face, with a small smile gracing his lips, kinder brown eyes, making him look slightly more approachable.

"Hey man, I'm Hunter" he introduced holding his fist out, I gave him a nod, tapping my fist with his. My subconscious geeking out that this was my first fist bump, I'm pathetic I know.I introduced my self quietly, awkwardly sitting down on the bench.

"Ever get the feeling of being watched?" I asked, my sarcastic side floating to the surface as I glanced behind me seeing everyone stare at me in shock. I've accomplished something that a lot have tried and failed, I was invited and I am sitting on their table.

Hunter chuckled as he continued to his lunch, I kept my eyes to my lap so my stomach didn't get any ideas. Gradually the sound in the cafeteria started to rise with chatter, most probably talking about me and why I'm sitting here, am I vain for thinking that?

Grace XOX

Chapter ~ 4

It's Okay || Gabriel Lewis

"Evening mother" I greeted letting the twins hands go, allowing them to rush into the room, I glanced over seeing my father, which shocked me slightly considering it's Wednesday. He looked old. His hair was greying, probably from all the stress, dark bags under his eyes from not having enough sleep, cheeks hollowed out, his skin pale.

My father has been a man of very few words when it comes to me, he barley acknowledges my presence let alone talks to me. In a way, I've lost both my parents years ago when this all started. I can't complain cause I know what my father is doing, he is working hard to keep the roof over our heads and the treatment for mother going, but sometimes I wish I had my father back and my mother.

Turning to my siblings, I got them set up in the corner with drawing and colouring their books that they got for their birthday. "I love you Gabe" Lilly said grinning up at me, I smiled, crouching beside her, ignoring the pain that erupted from my body, smiling softly at her, "I love you too Lilly" I replied pressing a kiss to her cheek, stretching my hand out to mess Jack's hair up, "I love you too Jack" I said laughing as he patted down his hair.

Turning my attention back to my parents, I sat in one of the chairs near the bed, listening into their hushed conversation, mindlessly. They were arguing about me and the twins.

"Anthony. I know your working hard, but they're your kids, they hardly see you. Gabriel doesn't get a day off either, he is taking care of the twins every day. Do you even know your children anymore?" Mother said weakly, coughing heavily.

"Sandra we are already in debt, I can't stop otherwise I'll can't afford for treatment . I do this for you!" Father grumbled, I glanced down, wishing that I could help out, to get a job, but the twins need me. What shocked me was the debt, I was never told that we actually owed money, I knew we were only scraping past with bills but I thought our heads were above water.

"I've stoped treatment" mother said, making my already damaged world crack more. My eyes staring at her with horror, treatment Is what keeps her alive, She can't last long with out it.

"You what?!" My father screamed angrily, his face red, hands balled into fists, as much as I wanted to be there for my mother and ask questions, the fearful eyes of my siblings became my main concern.

"Dad enough!" I snapped standing up finally, placing a hand on his shoulder, I couldn't bare to see my mother's tears. "Shut up boy!" He growled, I heard it before I felt it, a hand met my cheek with force, the slap echoed in the room.

I felt like I was doing the ice bucket challenge, as shock flooded my system. The force of my fathers backhand and look that followed was enough to shatter part of my world, there was no remorse or guilt, just anger. My life just goes from bad to worse.

"Lillian, Jack, wait for me out side okay? I'll be there in a minute" I said calmly glancing at my two siblings who looked terrified with tears streaming down their cheeks. "Leave your things" I added, they nodded as they scrambled out the room. They already saw too much.

Once the door shut, the betrayal and anger I so badly wanted to let out, was swallowed along with the emotion on my face. I turned to my away from my father walking around the other side of the bed, she had tears streaming down her cheeks, body shaking with sobs.

Leaning down I wrapped my arms around her, "it's okay Mum" I whispered, my heart was breaking with what I was going to say but I knew it was time. She was living on borrowed time, she wasn't enjoying life anymore, only surviving because of us. living without pain is something we should be entitled to do for as long as we can and we aren't giving her this by keeping her here. I knew this along time ago, I just didn't want to accept it.

"It's okay to leave" i whispered my voice cracking, hearing her heartbreaking sob. "I want you to be happy and pain free. So it's okay to stop fighting, it okay." I managed to croak out. Her fingers gripping my shirt tightly. "I'll take care of Lillian and Jack" I whisper tears finally slipping down my cheeks. Pressing my lips to her forehead before turning to face my father, who seemed to of calmed down, though all the trust I have in him is gone.

He looked heartbroken, the sadness in his broken eyes were clear to see. I think he knows as well that it's Mother's time to go, that keeping her here wouldn't be fair on her and to be honest she wouldn't last much longer.

I stepped back, walking to the door opening my arms for my siblings to run into. "It's time to say goodbye to mummy, okay?" I said with a lump in my throat, I needed to stay strong for them, I can't let them down. They needed me. They walked up to mother and gave her big hugs, Mum holding on tightly as she sobbed saying her goodbyes.

"Don't cry mummy, we will come back to see you soon" jack said inno-
cently, Lillian agreeing with him, "yeah mum, next time I'll show you my
dance" she added with a hopeful look in her watery eyes.

Jack was curled by my mother side closest to me, while Lillian was curled
on my lap, both sleeping peacefully. Mums hand was gripping mine as she
also was a sleep, only me and my father were awake, barely.

Tears had stoped hours ago, we weren't suppose to be here but the nurses
allowed us to stay with pitiful eyes. Not that I wanted it but I was thankful
we could stay. We had said our goodbyes, my world is already in a crumbling mess beyond repair, I had no more tears to be shed.

It was just past three in the morning when, the last bit of strength left her,
the last breath of oxygen that flowed through her body left. Her heart was
finally relived if it's duty's.

I grabbed my two disoriented siblings who were confused on what's happening, walking out of the room as nurses and doctors flooded in. I held
on to them tight as if they were going to leave me too, New tears streamed
down cheeks.

"Mummy isn't here anymore, is she?" Jack croaked out, his voice muffled
in my chest, I shook my head, "she is where she belongs" I croaked out,
placing my hand over his heart. "In our hearts" I whispered.

As the days pass in a blur, I managed to look like a normal person. I only
missed school on Thursday after I went to school; I took care of the twins
like always; my father worked. Nothing seemed really that important,
daily tasks were exhausting, dishes piled up in the sink, knives crusted with
strawberry jam.

Throughout this time, I experienced an acute nostalgia, a longing for a lost time that was so intense I thought it might split me in two, like a tree hit by lightning. I was flooded by memories - a submersion that threatened to overwhelm me, water coming up around my branches, rising higher. I yearned for the sound of her voice saying my name, telling me to 'lighten up'.

I found myself opening a cut on my arm and watching as the red drops of blood welled up. I did not want to hurt myself or die. I just wanted to create some symbol of the heartache that was eating me up. I was surprised by how physically taxing grief was.

In the past I had been good at keeping track of details, but now I couldn't. Often it took all my energy simply to get to school, and in class I found it hard to concentrate. Instead, my brain ran through my mother's last days over and over. I intensely wanted to write down the story of her death, scream it out for the world to hear, let them know they had lost an angel.

I kept coming back to a simple fact: my pain was caused by the absence of my mother. Did I want to deny this? Did I want to take something to make it go away? No. Grief is common. We know it exists all around us. But experiencing it made me suddenly aware of how difficult it is to confront head-on. When we do, it's usually in the form of self-help: we want to heal our grief.

There is no correct heal grief , there isn't one correct way of grieving, like there isnt one correct way of eating an Oreo.

Mainly, I thought: 'My mother is dead, and I want her back.' A mother is a story with no beginning; that is what defines her. What are you to do when the story ends?

With my mother's death, the person who brought me into the world left it, a door closing behind her, a line of knowledge binding her body to mine in the old ways. Who else contained me, felt me kick, nursed me? She crosses my mind like an exotic bird flying past the edge of your eye:

startling,

luminous,

lovely,

gone.

Chapter ~5

I nsight || Jaxon Coles

Blood pumped loudly in my ears, my right fist swinging upwards, hitting the side of my opponents jaw, my final blow being just under his rib cage.

Screaming assaulted my hearing as arms wrapped around my shoulders, bringing me out of what ever trance I get into when I'm fighting. I glanced to my right where Hunter stood, his hand wrapped around my wrist as he held it up with a grin on his face. Looking around at the screaming crowd, I let a smirk rise on my lips, hearing my name being chanted.

Daniel handed me four wads of cash, kept together with lackey bands. Four thousand dollars cash, for wining the fight and ten percent of the bets that were made tonight on top.

It was easy cash for less then thirty minutes work, apart from a few cuts, bruises and the occasional broken bone, I couldn't complain earning over four grand a night; 2 nights a week, cash in hand. No strings attached, the more consecutive wins, the higher you get on the board, the more money you win. Simple. Don't show, no money and you start again from the bottom.

The boss, Daniel, is a multimillionaire and has money to blow off so he started this unground, bordering illegal fight club of sorts in an abandoned car warehouse on the dark side of town, which has been turned into a fighting ring, and Gym. Every night from 9pm till midnight basically is fight night.

Since I've been fighting since I was fifteen, I've gotten to know Daniel, who to be honest isn't a bad guy. He took me under his wing, taught me all I know and basically gave me a job fighting. I get a grand for showing up, no mater if I win or not.

I gave him a nod before allowing hunter to pull me out of the cage, through the chanting crowd and into a private room with my name plastered on the door. Another wad of cash waiting for me, which as usual I hand over to hunter, since he trains me through the week and makes sure I don't die of infection.

He cleaned up my wounds to the best of his ability's, commenting that none are hospital worthy tonight. Hunter passed me a beer, commenting on my win, before both of us chugged the bottle. It was post fight routine.

"So Whats up with nerd boy?" Hunter asked curiously as we waited for Daniel. I looked up from my phone, shrugging. I really don't know why the hell I invited the kid to our table, stupid move really, he's gonna probably get it from James tomorrow.

Ive always wondered why James and the rest of the school were so adamant on making the kid's life a living hell, cause in reality, me and hunter are loners to, we don't have a cliché group to define us or a large group of friends, yet for some reason we are treated like royalty.

I almost feel sorry for him. Almost.

"I have an English project to with him. He ain't no use to me if he is dead" I replied, English is the one subject I have a hard time passing, i can't help it, I need to pass English if I want to graduate, part of the assignment is how we work together.

"Plus James is a try hard, dick-twat" I added, earning a laugh from Hunter. I don't play football but fuck, James can't play for shit, I swear the only reason that asshole is on the team is because his uncle is coach. His dad must be loaded with the amount of money he has to fork out to pay coach to keep twinkle toes as quarterback, let alone on the team.

Daniel walked a grin spreading on his lips, most clubs like this are usually illegal and gang related so entering them is risky and not that trustworthy. Daniel has a family and a business reputation to up hold so he can't afford the club to become associated with gangs and illegal activities unless it's far below the radar, like this club.

"Good fight out there kid" Daniel commented, patting my back a few times, making sure not to get to close to my chest as he didn't want to dirty his expensive suit. "Thanks old man" I replied with a smirk. Gathering my items, while listening to Daniel's chatter about the night and how it's going, falling into easy conversation with Hunter.

"Isn't that nerd boy?" Hunter mentioned half way though me talking, my eyes glanced as the side of the road as I drove past, he had two children, who I assumed were his siblings walking beside him.

My curiosity spiked slightly noticing the large bruise on his cheek, which I know he didn't revive through school hours, he wasn't there yesterday (Thursday) and Wednesday James kept his distance after the lunch scene. Which only leaves home, which didn't sit well in my stomach.

"Nasty bruise he has there, did James do that?" Hunter asked with his body turned to look back at him through the window as we drove past. "No. That didn't come out of school" I muttered, my fingers gripping the steering wheel a little tighter.

I couldn't stand parents that hurt their children, it was one thing that I hated with a passion, my mother had been abused by her father and no one ever noticed. My mother and father have opened our home to abused kids that needed fostering since I could remember, I've grown up with kids and their stories.

Parking in our usual spot, cheerleaders almost flocked to us, in futile hope that they could get into my pants. Pathetic the lot of them. Hunter has a girl already, not that he tells anyone, since it's no ones damn business and I'm still deciding on what I find more attractive, boobs or dicks.

We both ignored them, hoping that one day they will get the picture that we aren't interested in what ever cheep, artificial crap they have to offer. It's been three years and they have yet to figure it out, they seem to only getting more annoying.

Walking into the doors, I became Moses and parted the sea of students. Walking down the hall to my locker, Hunter leaning on his, which was next to mine. "Here comes lord farquaad and his herd of sheep" Hunter commented, making me groan, praying to what ever is up there for him not to talk to me.

"What the fuck man? What was that the other day?" He growled out, trying and failing to sound intimidating. Turning I looked at him, with a raised eyebrow, "are you questioning me?" I asked taking a step towards him, making the whole group step back. Honestly Pathetic, all I would have to do is glare and they all would be running off with their balls sucked up their asses and tails between their legs.

"I don't know if you got the memo, but I do what ever the fuck I want." I growled out, watching James' tough facade crumble into the weakling he is. "You are just my bitch, if I tell you to sit, you'll fucking sit until I tell you otherwise" I growled threateningly, my hands gripping his jacket, bringing his punch worthy face closer to mine

"if I tell you to leave him alone. I expect that you won't fucking touch him, or you'll answer to me" I growled glaring at him, letting him go, turning back to my locker continuing with getting my day ready. I honestly don't why I added the last part, concerning the nerd kid who I've yet to learn the name of. I figured he had enough abuse outside of school, plus it's about time James stoped with his bullying antics.

I was surprisingly anxious for English. Gabriel as the teacher announced, was a little late but showed up. Tear stained cheeks, blood shot eyes, blank stare and that fucking bruise on his cheek. "You look like shit man" I commented, my eyes narrowing at that stupid bruise which has been on my mind the whole day.

"close your eyes or look away" he replied a thin coat of sarcasm covering his words, making me chuckle. "So you gonna tell me who gave you the bruise?" I ended up blurting out, I honestly surprise my self at how insensitive I can sound, but then again most kids that come into my home are usually quiet open with it and I don't want to give of the impression that I care to the noisy arsewipes around me.

He looked up at me with broken eyes, I wonder if it has anything to do with him being in the hospital Monday night. "I didn't peg you down for listening to other people's sob stories" he replied rolling his eyes before staring back at his fingers.

"Well the whole point of this English assessment if to write about each other's sob stories, I figured we'ed leave the best for last." I bit back, leaning on the desk, trying to figure this dude out. He lets him self get basically walked over by everyone, not a peep for a comeback or anything to stand up for him self yet all I've gotten is attitude and sarcasm.

"If I'm going to tell you about my pathetic life, I'm not doing it here. I don't need give plankton and his pickle-brained minions another reason to make my life hell." He replied after a longish silence.

"Fine, my house after school. We can pick up your siblings on the way."

Chapter ~ 6

S lumber party || Gabriel Lewis

Jaxon Coles. Someone I typically wouldn't want to be in a 10 meter radius of, considering James and his minions were always close by and yet, here I am. In the back seat of a BMW, a car that I could only dream about and admire from afar. The drive took less then 5 minutes to get to the twins school, considering there was traffic.

Stepping out the car, I went to retrieve my reasons to continue living. They grinned when they saw me, running in my open arms, I ignored the pain lifting them from the ground for a few seconds, their giggles making my day a little brighter.

"I got a surprise for you two!" I said as I lead them to the car park, keeping quiet as they excitedly ask their questions about the surprise. I had to chuckle at some of the ideas they came up with. Lillian was convinced I got her a unicorn.

"You got us a car?!" Jack yelled excitedly, a large grin spread over his face, eyes lighting up, as we neared Jaxon's dark blue car, I let out a laugh, I wish. "No bud, not quiet" I replied opening the back door, "but you get to ride in one" I said chuckling at their excited squeals, almost happy that Jaxon offered, this is the excited and happiest I've seen them in a while.

"Move over, I have to fit as well" I chuckled at the two, who looked in complete awe of the car, Lillian grinned at me grabbing my hand and holding it tightly. "Your the best brother ever!" She said with a grin, jack voicing his agreement as he looked around the car interior.

"Guys, meet Jaxon who owns the car and Hunter" I introduced, chuckling as Jack jumped into all sorts of questions about the car. Lillian lifting my arm and wrapping around her shoulders, I smiled pressing a kiss to her head. Lilly was always excited and curious of cars but never a fan in actually riding in them, she had always been a bit uneasy with riding in a moving cars.

School was weird today. Well for me it was, my usual close encounters with floors, walls, lockers, and now James' fist and shoes, haven't happened at all today, I hardly heard an insult from James' mouth today with was extremely weird behaviour coming from him. I wondered what happened in the 24 hours I stayed locked up in my room.

Dad has yet to make an appearance at the house, I don't know where he is, cause he hasn't been home, usually I hear him come home but ever since Mum, he's been a no show. The twins don't fully understand what's happened with their mother, only knowing she isn't here anymore. The funeral is being held in a 2 week from now, I have no idea how we are going to pay for it. Funerals aren't cheep as we found out.

We arrived at Jaxon's apartment building, the garden looking more expensive then my house. The twins were completely awestruck at the place, looking around curiously. My eyes widened at the interior. How much money did Jaxon actually have? Either that or his parents have nice pay checks.

"Can I press the button please?!" Jack asked almost jumping out of his skin in excitement, elevators were another thing that the twins absolutely love to go in. Specially jack, he loves anything mechanical. "Sure thing kid" Jaxon chuckled lifting my brother so he could reach the correct floor, which was top floor.

"You're an excitable little boy aren't ya?" Hunter laughed, ruffing up his hair. "We never get to go in these things! Only when we visit mummy, but mummy's gone now." Jack rambled out looking around excitedly, saying way to much.

"Mummy's happy now, isn't she?" Lilly asked softly looking up at me, I smiled softly at her, blinking away tears. "Yeah, yeah she is Lilly" I muttered picking her up, placing her on my hip, ignoring the bruises that protested at the weight. I didn't look at the other two boys who I'm sure has put two and two together.

Jaxon's apartment was huge, modern and everything you'd expect from a rich kid. Large painting and wall Muriel's covered most the walls. The kitchen looked like it came out of an ikea magazine, the rest of the living looking spotless apart from a few articles of clothing thrown around the place. There was a pinball machine pushed up against the wall under the staircase. Damn it's nice.

"I'm guessing you like it?" Hunter laughed once again ruffing up Jack's hair, his eyes wide as he turned in circles looking around at the place. Lilly was awed too, looking wide eyed at everything but not leaving my side, her fingers gripping the back of my jumper. "This is so cool!" Jack yelled jumping up slightly, I have no idea where all his energy came from.

Hunter was automatically Jacks best friend since he showed him how to use the pinball machine. Lillian being a lot more timid then her brother stuck by me, glued to my arm.

Surprisingly we got through quiet a bit of the questions that we had to prepare. Both going back and forth, neither of us really got into personal stuff cause honestly it's no ones business. Jaxon ordered take out for dinner which jack was completely mind blown that the food was delivered to the door. I promised him that I would pay him back which he waved it off.

"So what did you do to get on James' bad side?" Hunter asked, handing me a glass of water. I've been here for a few hours now, Jack is completely worn out, laying on the couch with his head on my lap asleep. Lilly was sitting between in front of my legs, drawing on some paper that Jaxon gave her.

"Im just unlucky I guess" I said shrugging, I really want to believe that James doesn't completely hate my existence because of my sexuality. "That sucks my-dude." Hunter said shaking his head as he took a sip of his beer.

"So where did the bruise come from?" Jaxon asked once again narrowing his eyes on my bruised cheek. Why he cares or wants to know is beyond me, he asked me this before in school. I hoped that he would leave it and ignore it, I guess not.

"I slipped" I lied which Jaxon didn't believe for a second, snorting loudly before calling bullshit. "Your father hit you, didnt he?" Jaxon asked with an unreadable expression, how in gods name did he come to that correct conclusion?

"you didn't get that in school, James' ego was to hurt on Wednesday, Thursday you didn't show up, today you had it before you were in school grounds. Its a common thing, mother dies, father gets abusive" Jaxon explained his reasoning, which was slightly weird why he paid that much attention to me in the first place.

"She died yesterday, you insensitive prick" I snapped, glancing down at Lilly who was looking at me with tearful eyes. "Mummy isn't coming back from the happy place is she?" She asked softly, my heart broke for her.

"Lill, you remember that drawings you made of mummy on the rainbow?" I asked her pulling her up to my free side, she nodded sniffling. I smiled softly wiping her tears, "well sweet heart, she's there now, she's riding the rainbows." I explained softly wrapping an arm around her. The afternoon was going so well, why did have to end in tears.

They still can't fully comprehend that their mother is gone and not coming back, it's honestly heartbreaking and I know it's going take a while before they understand that she won't come back.

Jaxon looked slightly guilty staring at Lilly and my self. Hunter looked came over with a teddy in his hands, which i didn't even notice he left the room. "Hey princess" he said softly tapping her shoulder, crouching in front of her, "this is Pete, his Mum went to the happy place too" Hunter explained holding the stuffed bunny rabbit, "do you think you could look after him? he needs a home" hunter said smiling softly when she nodded, cuddling the rabbit close to her chest.

"Me and hunt already had one too many drinks to drive legally, and your definitely not walking home with those two at this time of night." Jaxon said gulping down the last of his beer, I raised an eyebrow at him, is he suggesting that I stay the night? Confirming my thoughts when he offered the guest bedroom.

"I'll grab the vodka and nail polish. ka-bam we have a slumber party." Hunter added grinning, waving his arms around, I laughed at his actions, Lilly giggles muffled by the rabbit.

I sighed knowing I don't have much choice considering I wouldn't know my way home from here anyway. Wrapping my arms around my brother, I picked him up, cradling him to my chest. Lilly giggled in Jaxon's arm as he picked her up and placed her on his shoulders. "Look gabe, Im taller then you!" She said through her giggles, reaching out to pat my head.

Jaxon offered up his own bed, mentioning he deserved a night on the couch for making Lilly cry. So in other words it was an apology, I chuckled feeling slightly weird that I was taking Jaxon Coles bed, but accepted the offer, he showed me the bathroom and grabbed a few pieces of clothing for me like he did for the twins, he had kid clothing from when family come over and visit.

Jaxon Coles must have one of the most comfortable beds in the world cause holy moly I was out before my head reached the pillow.

Chapter ~7

F ired || Gabriel Lewis

   I was woken by a body curling up with mine and small giggles, opening my eyes I saw the fuzzy picture of Jack laying next to me with a large grin and Lilly sitting on the edge of the bed. I chuckled wrapping my arms around Jack making him squeal, I laughed pressing kisses to his face as he squirmed to get out of my grip.

"Gabe! We had a sleep over!" Jack said excitedly as he held his arms out to stop my attack of kisses, his hands holding my face carefully so he wouldn't hit the bruise. "I know we did bud. Cool eh?" I said thanking Lilly for handing me my glasses making the world around me clear once more.

They pulled me out of bed saying they helped make me breakfast, I chuckled allowing them, I didn't have a shirt on, only some sweatpants that were slightly to big. They didn't even allow me to get a shirt before I was out the door, my torso was full of bruises for the world to see.

"Look Gabe! Look! We made pancakes!" Jack yelled excitedly pointing at plate of pancakes in the table, decorated with melted chocolate chips that resembled something of a smiley face. Pulling my arms in, which resulted in my sibling stumbling together, "thank you for this beautiful breakfast" I mumbled my arms wrapping around their waists tightly before I pressed kisses to there cheeks making them once again squeal.

"I smell.." hunter started as he entered the room, with out missing a beat Jack replied 'yeah you do' before bursting out in a fit laughter, Lilly giggled along watching hunter raise an eyebrow, a playful smirk rising on his lips,

"What was that little punk?" He asked walking slowly towards up. Jack eyes widened as hunters wiggling fingers, untangling him self from my hold and running off, his giggle following him.

While jack was in laughing fits begging for hunters tickling mercy, Lilly offered her help with placing the cutlery on the table while my offer to help was declined. Only then did I notice Jaxon was very much like me, shirtless. Well Hot damn that boy has a nice body and a few tattoos.

Once breakfast was served, my mouth watered at the sight of the pancakes and bacon in front of me, we haven't had a proper breakfast in years. This breakfast didn't disappoint, it was delicious, the kids were for once quiet, as they enjoyed their breakfast.

I couldn't help but be thankful, Jaxon invited me into his home, allowing my siblings to come too. Both Jaxon and hunter have been nothing below amazing with Lilly and Jack, I haven't seen them smile and laugh like this in a long time. Jaxon gave up his extremely comfortable bed and fed us, proper meals.

To be honest, the scary dynamic duo that rules the school, weren't all that the rumours say about them, they both are completely different to what I was expecting. Contrary to popular belief, Jaxon can talk and hold a decent conversation. Hunter entertained the kids and cracked a joke a few times. I can't say I didn't have a good time, cause I had a wonderful time. I'm almost sad that I have to go home.

"Can we stay here forever?! It's fun here!" Jack asked looking at me with hopeful eyes, I chuckled shaking my head "sorry bud" I muttered pushing the empty plate forward slightly. "You're welcome to come by anytime" Hunter offered, nudging jack with his elbow. "Can I come tomorrow? And the next day?!" Lilly joined the conversation, with a large grin, chocolate covering her mouth and teeth, her twin didn't look much better.

Jaxon let out a laugh, which I almost melted to but quickly extinguished my mind's thoughts, "come on you two, let's get you cleaned up." I muttered, feeling self conscious of my body under Jaxon's stare.

"Bathroom is connected to my room, it has a shower and bath which ever you prefer, feel free" Jaxon said shrugging, I cringed as he said bath. "You have a bath?! Can we take a bath please?!" Both my siblings started begging with wide excited eyes. We have a bath it just doesn't work and no one would want to go near it nor touch it with a ten foot pole.

I sighed in defeat, while my sibling cheered, once again dragging me up the stairs. Hunter and Jaxon's laugher echoing through the room. When Jaxon said bath he meant hot tub, with Bubbles and coloured lights. Jaxon came in a few minutes later with towels and a spare set of clothing for both of them. Turning on the 'bath' for us as I had no clue. While he got that ready, I wiped clean the faces of my siblings with damp paper towel.

"So shall we have the pink Bubbles or green?" Jaxon asked holding up two bath bombs, jack could hardly contain his excitement at the fact there was a bath bomb to be used, so Lilly got to choose which was pink. My siblings were easy to entertain as they watched the water and foamy Bubbles turn pink. He was smart and left, so I could deal with the task of giving them a bath. Does he know how hard it is to shower these kids? Let alone give them a bath of their wildest dreams.

After successfully getting them clean and not completely flooding the bathroom, i managed to get them out of the bath, which was a mission by its self. They both smelled like strawberry's and coconut, which I didn't mind, I helped drying them off and re clothing them into the clothes that Jaxon so kindly gave. Which amazingly fit perfectly.

Jack was wearing jeans and a white polo shit, looking like a mini heartbreaker with his hair slicked back or that he is off to play golf. Lilly looked like a princess wearing a floral dress that came just above her knees, with thermal white tights underneath to keep her warm.

After they were finished, I sent them off so I could have a shower, a nice steaming hot shower, just how I like it. Getting out my skin was bright red, drying and dressing my self in Jaxon's clothes which are slightly to big on me.

Home. It was honestly embarrassing, I wished the ground would eat me up whole, as we turned into the street, the houses going from bad to worse, until you reached mine, the house before the one that is half fallen down.

When Jaxon stopped in my driveway, the kids were already thanking him before managing to get out of the car with out any limbs getting stuck in closing door. "Thank you Jaxon, for last night and this morning" I said after a small silence.

I watched as my front door opened showing my dad, who looked horrible with a beer in his hand, pale face unshaven face. "Gabriel do you have a phone?" Jaxon asked narrowing his eyes at my father. I shook my head watching my siblings walk in the house. I use to but I had to sell if for a few bucks to by a present for the twins.

"If anything happens. Call Hunter" Jaxon said handing me a sleek newest iphone. I glanced at the phone sighing, I highly doubt Dad would hit me again, it was a one time thing right? My Dad's not abusive.

"My dad isn't abusive" I said, hating my voice for coming out unsure. A rough hand griped my chin, turning my face to look at him. "That is abuse" he muttered his thumb brushing over the healing bruise on my cheek.

I sighed pulling away, keeping his phone in hand, thanking him once again, getting out of his car, his phone in my hand. "That's a nice looking phone boy" my father said as I stepped into the house.

I glanced up at him, he didn't look like my father, his voice was rough and unkind, his eyes were broken and he was drinking beer. My father never drank.

"It's my friend's phone" I replied placing my school bag down. "Dad what are you doing?" I asked motioning to his unkept self. Mums gone, we all know that and feel that but we all have responsibilities still.

I look after the twins, Dad works and is there for us when he can. Now mums gone, it should let us save some money, get us out of the debt that I never knew we were in.

"Don't criticise me boy! Where were you last night?" He yelled, his words slightly slurred, I sighed glancing at the living which looked like a hurricane came through a bottle shop. "Dad we all miss Mum. Drinking isn't going to bring her back. The twins need their father, I need my father. So please stop with this" I said pleadingly.

Mum is gone, that's one support system that I don't have,I don't need my father to go down the same road, I can't do this by my self. I have school, I want to get somewhere in life, I want my future kids to live in a proper house and not have to worry about the next meal. I want to do something with mine so the twins can follow their dreams. I know I'm not much but I hope I can get somewhere in the world which isn't here.

My father looked at me blankly, no emotion in his lifeless grey orbs. "I got fired six months ago from the fuel station." He admitted a sardonic laugh leaving his lips. Well that answers why we are in debt, if he hasn't been working for the fuel station most nights then what has he been doing? The fuel station was our main pay check. The other jobs he has dosnt get him very much, they were all cash under the table jobs, but it was money, even if it was illegal.

Grace XOX

Chapter ~ 8

F urious || Gabriel Lewis

Mother Nature is a Regina George. It poured down all weekend having small spots of wet snow but for the most part it was raining, sadly unlike The Weather Girls's song 'raining men' it was only water, cold water that leaked all through the house. On the bright side I found a use for all the empty beer bottles.

Nothing much happened, I completed some homework including the English assignment, father left the house in the morning but I'm not completely sure on if he went to his weekend work down at the abattoir, he hasn't stoped drinking which worried me as he has been very vocal, which I can handle but the twins not so much.

Last night Mother Nature decided to give the reins to Elsa as it snowed heavily the whole night, the twins didn't bother going to their own beds, climing straight into mine with long pants and comfy jumpers on to battle the cold, I did the same, wearing Jaxon's sweatpants that if I'm honest I lived in for the past two days, and a jumper.

How I wished I was in Jaxon's warm, comfortable bed, not my own cheep old uncomfortable thing. The snow didn't let up in the morning, I wasn't even sure how we would make it to school and back. Our winter clothes and shoes aren't the best of quality so we would be soaked and most likely frozen by the time we got there.

A ringtone sounded loudly by my bedside table, scaring me half out of my skin, looking over I noticed Hunters name flash across the screen. Grabbing the phone I slid my finger over the screen, before bringing the phone up to my ear. "be ready in an hour" Jaxon said before the line went dead, I didn't even get a hello in. Be ready for what? Is he going to pick me up? Why though?

Usually I would need to leave in 10 minutes, specially in this sort of weather to get to school on time. The phone buzzed again explaining in text that he would be picking me up for school, which I was thankful for since I'm definitely not going to walk in this weather.

"Why are you still here boy?" My father grumbled walking in, a new six pack of beer in his hands. Pushing the door shut with some force before it slammed, rattling the windows slightly.

"My friend is driving me" I answered slightly weary of my father, he never usually calls me boy, it was alway son, or my name. Never boy, seems like that's the only name he knows since mother died. Grumbling under his breath, he walked past me, bumping into my shoulder as he made his way to the couch. "Dont you have work?" I asked knowing that his shift at the car yards would have already started. Snow never stoped him before. "I quit" he grumbled.

My head was spinning. What the hell! The day work at the slaughterhouse is not going pay all the bills or put food on on the table, specially with him waisting money on beer. "Are you serious right now?!" I yelled fuming at the man who is not only throwing his life away but endangering his kids.

"We are in debt and you decide to quit your job? Are you fucking with me right now?" I growled, swearing for the first time since forever. "We are in financial debt, you lost your last job. Two things you never thought to tell me! So your answer to this is quit your other job and waist the money we could be spending on surviving another day on beer!" I yelled furious at him. How dare he! I don't get to grieve over my mother and throw my life away, so my father sure as hell cant.

"Mums gone! She is never coming back! If she did she would be disgusted! You are pathetic! We all miss her, she was important to us as well you know. Pull your self together before you lose your children too!" I threatened, I don't how but I will take my siblings away from my father if he doesn't get his act together, I will not let them watch and think that turning to alcohol is the answer.

I was to slow to react, the punch to my cheek, knocked me off my feet. My jaw throbbed painfully, my heart dropped knowing that the father I once knew is no longer there, once was an accident, second time is a choice. The pain in my heart was the same pain when I lost my mother, cause I know I lost my father too that day. He is gone and there is nothing I can do apart from do what I've always done and have vowed to always do. Take care of my siblings.

There was no remorse or guilt in his eyes, he didn't care. I was nothing to him at the moment. Tears sprung to my eyes, not from the pain of the punch but the feeling of my life falling apart, the foundation that I once had under my feet is crumbling and falling away.

I'm only 17, i don't have a job or a savings that I saved up cause all my money went to my siblings. Apart from this wreak of a house, I have no where to go, I don't have friends and even if I did I couldn't ask them to take me and my siblings in.

I stood up and walked away, my eyes meeting the fearful teary eyes of my sibling. Leading them to their rooms I told them softly to pack their bags. I don't know where Ill go but here isn't safe anymore. Grabbing my other backpack I packed a few pieces of clothing, which was already limited and a few other things that I could possibly sell.

I grabbed the photo album from my dads room. Since it had all baby photos and happy memories, I also found a few wads of cash. Which made me more furious, so I took 3 wads of cash, not caring at least it will go to good use instead of beer, and my mother's favourite necklace. Stuffing it all in my bag. Jaxon's phone buzzed which was a text saying they were here.

I grabbed the twins, quickly wiping their tears, "don't cry, we are going to go an adventure okay? Just like buzz light year" I said, managing a fake grin, they nodded walking into my arms for a hug. "Come on Jaxon's outside" I whispered which did the trick in getting them excited, well Jack at least. Holding their hands I quickly ushered them to the door, grabbing my school bag by the door. I opened it telling them to go to the car, which was a huge black pickup truck. (Ute)

"Don't expect us back. I will not allow you to ruin their lives because you can't handle yours. Good bye Anthony" I stated before slamming the door closed. I trudged through the snow towards the truck that Jaxon was standing by the door.

He didn't say anything when I got to him, only grabbing my arm, halting me from getting in the car. His other hand coming up to brush my jaw. Shaking his head before allowing me to jump in.

Lilly curled into my side almost immediately, tears streaming down her innocent face. My arm wrapped around her shoulders, my hand gripping Jack's shoulder. "I'll always be your brother, but I'll raise you as my own." I promised quietly, their tearful eyes staring up at me.

It didn't occur to me that we weren't going to school, not that I feel like going anyway, I have bigger things to handle. When we stopped, I recognised that we were at Jaxon's apartment complex, I'm assuming hunter is his room mate.

We all got out wordlessly, my head running through every possible idea on how to manage my self and take care of my siblings. When we got into the beautiful apartment, hunter ushered the kids to the guest room.

Placing my bags by the door, my legs gave out, as all the bottled up emotion that I've been keeping with in me, finally broke the barriers.Sobs wreaked my body as the last week come crashing down on my shoulders. Arms wrapped around my shoulders, bringing me into a hard chest.

"The sun always shines after a storm. The storm might last days, weeks, months or years but no matter what the sun will shine after every storm" Jaxon muttered his arms tightening around my body, as my arms snake around his waist. Holding to only thing that seems to not crumble at my touch.

"Fall apart Gabriel"

Hell must be having an ice age cause that is exactly what I did, in the arms of Jaxon Coles.

Chapter ~ 9

Stronger|| Gabriel Lewis

Days blurred together, not knowing really what day it was. I just continued. I thought the grief of losing my mother was hard, the added grief of losing my father who is alive but a ghost of his former self, plus the responsibilities of taking care of two children and not to mention my self, I was getting crushed. All this happens in the span of just over a week. I lost everything I knew, all foundations and support systems.

Ive lost a lot but also gained something I never thought ever get to claim as my own. Friends. Two amazing humans that I don't have any idea how or why but they have become my support systems.

The two rulers of the school, said to be heartless criminals have welcomed me and my luggage in their home with out much of a second thought, made the twins laugh and smile, picked me up when I broke apart. I don't want to know what Or where I'd be if it wasn't for them.

Hunter has become Jacks best friend, both as immature as each other and the energy levels to match. Jack is basically Hunters shadow, following him everywhere and doing everything that Hunter allows him help out on, which is almost everything. Those two are either planing world domination together or watching Disney. There is no in between.

Lilly is still trying to figure out everything and come to terms with everything that has happened. She has opened up quiet a bit and let her shy but cheeky personality come out sometimes, but is the complete opposite of her twin. She has taken a liking to the kitchen, cooking and baking anything that Jaxon decides to make.

School is extremely different, No one touches me now as I have two bulky body guards that are usually right next to me. They double up as In class entertainment, since I've found that Hunter is in most of my classes and the three he isn't, Jaxon is usually in.

So I can't really complain about my life at the moment well apart from the stupid feelings that are starting poke at my heart. Jaxon has and continues to be my glue supplier, every time I break down and fall apart, he is there with his arms around me, sweet nothings murmured in my ear. Im blaming the feelings for the boy on me being unstable emotional wreak and that he has a drool worthy body.

"Yo What do you call a lesbian dinosaur?" Hunter asked smirking at me, we were working through a practice exam for economics, well I was. I glanced at him with a raised eyebrow, glancing down at his completed economics mock exam, damn he was finished already?

"A lick-lotta-puss" he continued grinning at his joke, I rolled my eyes at the crude joke, laughing along with his contagious laughter. "What do you call the useless piece of skin on a dick?" I asked with a smirk, watching Hunters laughter dry up looking surprised at the makings of a crude joke. He shrugged raising an eyebrow.

"The man"

It was small, there was a few friends, work colleagues and some family who managed to come, not that their presence would be missed if they didn't show. My father has yet to show up, I have mixed emotions if i want him here or not.

A familiar face that I didn't expect to show was Claire, she walked up to me, her parents in tow. "I'm so sorry for your loss Gabe" She said softly, I nodded giving a weak smile as she hugged me. My confusion on why she was here was quickly cleared up when her mother mentioned being part of the same book club.

Jaxon walked up to me, pulling me into a tight hug, which I gave back, gripping the back of his suit, allowing a few tears to escape. Pulling back he flashed me a sad smile before turning to the older couple behind him, I guessed was his parents since the man looked like a carbon copy just older.

"Come here my child" the woman whispered pulling me into her warm embrace, I blinked not expecting it but returned the hug. "A friend of Jaxon, is a child of mine." The lady said softly, holding me tightly, i felt like falling apart in her arms, the lump in my throat getting harder to swallow. "If you ever need anything, advise, a motherly embrace, a night off from being big brother. Holly Coles at your service okay darling." Holly said smiling softly at me as she wiped the tears that managed to escape.

Jaxon's father Kane, patted my shoulder and introduced him self and the teenagers behind him as Max and Christine who I'm guessing were the foster children that Jaxon mentioned.

Hunter arriving a few minutes later with a beautiful girl on his arm. "hey bro" he greeted giving me a hug before introducing his long term girlfriend of 2 years Tara. She was sweet and very soft spoken, a little bit like Lilly.

Hunter's mother and step dad introduced them selves to me, mentioning if I needed anything that they would be happy to help.

It blew my mind that people who don't know me or my mother have come by and offered their support and help. Much more then my own family, hell my father.

I felt like I was thrown back to the hospital, having to relive the final heart breaking moments. As the ceremony started, Lilly's thumb once again in her mouth, something she hasn't done in a long time.

Jaxon's arm was wrapped around my shoulders as silent tears streamed down my cheeks. I honestly don't know what I would do with out Jaxon, who helped out with planing the funeral and paying for more then half of it, which I'm determined to pay him back.

The sun shined brightly in the sky which was a complete contradiction to what I was feeling. The pastor said a small prayer before it was my time to talk, I read out the Letter that I wrote over the past few days. My voice was cracking and sobs interrupted my speech quiet a bit, but I got through it, my siblings running up to me, half way through which didn't help my case at all, not that I would have it any other way.

Crouching down I hugged them tightly, repeating my promise over and over. Lilly and Jack said their final goodbyes as they lowered the casket. Jaxon held on to me as my world once again crashed down around me once again. I'm honestly sick of crying which I seem to be doing everyday, I feel sorry for Jaxon who has to deal with my emotional break downs.

After I calmed down, wiping the never ending streams of tears. People bid their goodbyes and condolences before leaving. Holly once again pulled me into a hug where i broke down once again. I honestly need to get a grip. I thanked her for comforting my siblings and making sure they were okay while I was breaking down in her son's arms.

Once everyone left, Hunter took jack and Lilly to the apartment. While I stayed behind sitting down at the grave stone of my mother. My father was a no show and if he did show up, he never made it known. I couldn't believe what my father has turned into, I hope that maybe he will comeback, become the father he once was.

I felt Jaxon sit beside me, placing an arm around my shoulders. "You know, you're stronger then you think" Jaxon commented after a long, peaceful silence. I glanced up at him with a raised eyebrow. Pointing to his shoulder "your suit has permanent water damage because of me" I argued, which made him chuckle.

"Crying doesn't make you weak Gabriel. She is your mother, I would be concerned if you didn't cry." He said tightening his arm around my shoulders pulling me into his side. "Your strong cause through all of this, you are still here, you haven't once given up, or backed down cause it was too hard. Your so much stronger then your father."

Dear Mum,

I want to thank you.

Thank you for being the best possible mother a child could have. You showed me compassion, generosity, love and support. You've scolded me when I was wrong and shown me the correct path. You've pushed me to be the best person I possibly could be, you pushed me to become someone like you. So thank you for being the best role model a child could have.

Jack and Lillian are easily the two of the greatest gifts you've given me. They are my shining stars when the world seems dark, my rocks that keep me grounded. I promised you when they were born that I would be the best big brother to them, I would protect them, love them and support them in what ever they do. That's a promise I will keep until I join you.

Now your gone, I will continue to be their big brother, but I'll raise them as my own, hoping to give them the same love, generosity, compassion and support that you've shown me. I will remind them and show them who you were and make sure your teaching are instilled in their hearts so they can grow up to be just like their mother. If I could just be only half the guardian that you were, I would be more than content with it.

I love you mother, may you Rest In Peace, and your soul and memory live on, supporting me, Lillian and Jack through our lives.

Lots of love, Lillian, Jack & Gabriel.

Chapter ~ 10

C uriosity || Jaxon Coles

Just over a month. It's been just over a month and I'm a goner. Maybe I feel sorry for him; maybe it's the way he is with his siblings; maybe it's his greyish eyes; maybe it's because he isn't interested; hell maybe its Tyler Joseph fault. Who knows what the reason is, all I know is that I'm a goner.

Lilly was as usual helping me out with dinner, she loves to help in the kitchen even though she slows me down, but it's fine cause she is cute doing it. She throws all her concentration into cutting vegetables or doing what ever else she does, it's quiet cute, at least I know she won't cut her self, though I'm always watching, just in case.

"All done sweet pea?" I asked softly seeing all the spring onion were cut up, she nodded happily, a proud grin on her face. I find it hilarious how Lilly is the complete opposite of her twin, Jack who just runs a muck with Hunter.

"Yep! What can I do next?!" She asked glancing around, as she stepped off the box. I chuckled, pointing to the table which needs setting, nodding she grabbed one plate at a time bring it to the table and coming back for the next. I continued to mix the vegetables and mince into the bolognese sauce.

Gabriel was completing homework, probably in his room which he is sharing with the twins. I know he has been trying to find a job, since he feels bad not contributing, he mentions that he will pay me back and get out of my hair, meaning move out. In all honesty I don't mind having him and the twins around.

I've always liked having full houses, I'm use to kids screaming and a lot of people in the house, that's what I grew up with, having a constant flow of foster children, most of them come back so my parents house was always full, it's basically a foster house.

I moved out because I needed my own space so Mum and Dad got me this apartment when I was fifteen, hunter moved in with me and I was a happy boy, I got money from fighting which my parents know nothing about, they think I work in a gym, which is partly true.

It confuses me why so many people dislike Gabriel at school, his sexuality is really none of their business and doesn't define who he is. For the same token, if no one likes him, it's more for me. Again I have no idea where these feeling come from but my heart has decided that Gabriel Lewis is mine and mine alone.

This should honestly be freaking me out, but I can't find it in me to care. I've always been curious about sexuality, It's such taboo subject within school and when I grew up around my grandparents, though my parents are completely accepting since we've had loads of Lgbtq foster kids, we have recently been to a wedding of a girl we took in, she's married to a transgender male.

Over the past few years I've had my one night stands with both genders, seeing what I clicked with and honestly none of them were particularly memorable. I never had a real sexual attraction to either gender or an urge to be with anyone romantically well that's until Gabriel came around, spinning me out completely.

You'd think the school has come to terms with the duo becoming a trio after the first few weeks of Gabriel sitting with us, I honestly thought he would earn a bit of respect. Neither happened, people still looked completely mindfucked at the sight of Gabe hanging around with Hunter and myself.

The only person who seems not to care is a chick called Claire, a cheerleader for the basketball team, weirdly enough she ain't a artificial barbie doll and is actually a nice human being.

It was good though, James and his crew of spineless dimwits haven't got the balls to confront Gabe with hunter and myself nearby, the most they do is glare and mutter under their breaths which I could care less about.

Walking through the halls, Gabe talked happily with Hunter about an economics test that they had coming up. Hunter is a smart guy, not that you would guess since he acts like a five year old half the time. That's is a reason why him and Jack get on so well, they both have matching mental maturity levels.

Hunter continued to walk with Gabe to his locker while I stoped at mine, grabbing the things I needed. "I made you into the person you are today and this is the thanks I get. You hang out with fagboy" James' snarled in my ear.

My fingers were around his neck in seconds, his body getting slammed into Hunter's locker with a loud bang. "I owe you nothing, you did fuck all. all you've been is an annoying little shit that doesn't fucking get the message to leave me alone" I growled, his face turning red from the lack of oxygen. "His name is Gabriel and I'll hang out with who the fuck i want. So back the fuck off. " I added before letting him go, resulting in him collapsing to the floor coughing and spluttering like a drowning cat.

Closing my locker I walked away, leaving the gaping fish to his his servants to fuss over him like flies to a piece of shit. I damn hope for this sake that he backs off and leaves me alone cause I'm gonna put the basted in hospital with more brain damage then he already has.

"You know violence isn't the answer" Gabriel said sitting beside me, I glanced at me before rolling my eyes "he deserved it" I reasoned not that he will buy it as a viable excuse. I assumed correct hearing the loud sigh of defeat. We have had this conversation a few times now.

"My Dad is looking for me apparently" he admitted softly, my fists tighten. Never met the guy and to be honest I really don't want to, with emotional stress and pain he has caused Gabe, he sounds like a someone my fist would love to meet.

"He can keep looking" I grumbled, getting a small smack in return, "Gabe, he hit you, twice. Basically abandoned you and the twins and didn't even bother to show up at the funeral. All of which is his fault, he let grief ruin his life, you didn't. Don't let him ruin it now" I said, which succeeded in getting him to think, I don't know where this caring, compassionate side came from. Stupid feelings.

"He is still raised me Jax, I can't just throw away fifteen of love away. He lost his wife of twenty five years, I mean that's gotta mess you up, right? The second time he had alcohol in his system, no one thinks straight drunk " Gabriel said, he sounded like he was trying to convince him self then argue a point.

"It's your decision Gabe, I can't stop you from doing anything, I will advise you and give you my option but it's up to you to decide what you will do." I said gripping his shoulder softly, he nodded biting his bottom lip.

Fuck me.

Literally, please do. Looking away from his pretty face, as self control came barging in, making sure I don't completely fuck up. "You do you, just know you not doing alone. Like fuck will I let you near that man alone, I don't care who he is" I added watching the small smile appear on his face in the corner of my eye.

Fuck. I'm turning into a hormonal teenage girl in a cheesy romance novel. Stupid heart.

The day dragged on, I was called to the Dean's office just before lunch, I had a suspicion that it was for the incident this morning. Arriving in the office my suspicions were proven correct seeing the back of his ugly head.

"Mr Coles, sit down" Mr Rodgers grumbled, his overweight ass sitting slouched in the office chair, leaning forward on his chubby arms. Dropping down on a seat I raised an eyebrow, glancing at the red finger prints around James' neck, a smirk rising on my lips. Good he might remember my threat this time.

"Mr Hiller has evidence with witnesses that you strangled him this morning" Rodgers mumbled, wiping his nose on his sleeve as he leaned backs "Is this true Mr Coles?" The fat ass looked at me with disapproving eyes.

"Strangled is a big word sir, he would be dead if i did that. If your asking if we had a bit of a disagreement this morning then, sure. We did" I replied, my smart mouthed reply apparently wasn't appreciated. Fat and no sense of humour, must be a 40 year old virgin.

"Mr Coles we do not tolerate violence or bullying-" that statement made me laugh, interrupting his bullshit filled speech. "No bullying? Golden boy here is the biggest bully in this school." I said, ignoring James' glare.

"He's been verbally and physically tormenting a student for years, as well has his team of dimwits. Twinkle toes is only playing victim cause he is butt hurt that I won't join him. The scuffle this morning, that he started, was me repeating myself to back off." I said truthfully, watching the hippo gape, James started to argue his point angrily standing up.

"Sit your ass down, you spineless toad"

Chapter ~ 11

Lessons || Gabriel Lewis

Driving a car, something I've done once before, it was when we still had our old station wagon, dad allowed me to sit on his lap and I could steer the car around the block. That was seven years ago. Six years ago money became tight, Mum was pregnant with the twins so the car was the first thing to go, to give us a bit of spare change to get ready for the new arrivals.

That old rust bucket would probably be worth a grand if your lucky, now I'm in the drivers seat of a BMW that is worth more then my old house and education put together.

So you can imagine, I was anything but calm and collected. I was sweating bullets and gripping the steering wheel like it was my life line so they wouldn't shake. "Don't worry so much, all you have to worry about is your foot and steering" Jaxon said leaning back in the seat, his hand on the hand brake.

"Is your foot on the brake?" Jaxon asked, I looked at him with a blank stare, "middle pedal, right foot" he added. I nodded, "good now press the start button and the car will turn on"

I pressed the button, the dash board flashing with lights before the all screens loaded and turned on. "See your already half way there. Now put the car in drive" he said pointing to the joy stick with letters lit up beside it. Why do I feel like London right now?

"Now, I'm going to lower the handbrake. Keep your foot on the brake. The car won't move. Alright" Jaxon said lowering the lever, keeping hold of it as he instructed to lift my foot off the brake slowly.

Me being the nervous wreak lifted my foot a bit to quickly making the car go forward at a quicker pace then I was expecting. In a panic my hands left the steering wheel to my chest. Jaxon pulled the hand brake on, making the car come to a sudden stop.

"Nope. I can't. I can't do it, I'm going to crash and destroy your expensive car. Nope not happening" I rambled, shaking my head, I tried and it's not for me. Not today. "Are you finished?" Jaxon said laughing, his deep melodic laugh echoing through the car. I pouted, nodding my head.

"Firstly, You hardly went two miles an hour, which you can walk faster then that. Secondly, never let go of the steering wheel" Jaxon said grabbing my hands and bringing them to the steering wheel once again.

"Now you did fine. So let's go again, slowly with the brake this time." He ordered softly leaving no room for my protests. I huffed placing the money pit in drive once more and doing it again, this time slowly.

I don't know where Jaxon's patience's came from because he definitely didn't have it in school. His voice stayed soft, not a drop of annoyance, as he repeated the same few steps over and over, no mater how many times I stuffed up and pulled my hands away from the wheel, he just gripped them put them back and start again.

Surprisingly, within an hour, I was driving,I dare say, confidently around the car park, a grin plastered on my lips as I drove. I wasn't going fast by any means but I was driving. By my self.

Jaxon took over, driving us into town, mentioning we needed a few things from the shops. We parked at the local mall, that had a few shops and cafes. Jaxon's mother Holly was babysitting the twins for us, allowing me to have some much needed time to my self, something I haven't been able to do for years. I almost felt weird not having my siblings by my side.

Dragging me to a small coffee shop, for a drink and some food. "Have you made up your mind about your father?" Jaxon asked, leaning forward on the table, placing his car keys, phone and wallet in front of him.

My father is looking for me apparently, Claire mentioned it to me that he was calling around for me. I didn't know what to do really, I wanted to believe that he cleaned up his act but the relationship between us will never be the same, he hit me, twice. The trust I had isn't there and quiet frankly I was scared. Scared of being disappointed by him. Again.

"I don't know." I mumbled playing with the straw mindlessly. A hand covered mine making me glance up at Jaxon. "You aren't alone anymore Gabriel. You got me and Hunter, hell my mother adores you already so you don't have to anything alone anymore." Jaxon said softly, gripping my hand softly. My heart almost bounced out my chest, ugh stupid boy, why is he being so damn sweet.

"I know jax, so thank you. Thank you for everything you've done and continue do for me and the twins. I owe you my life." I thanked him graciously, meaning every word. He smiled shaking his head "it's what friends are for"

Friends

My heart cracked a little at the word.

Slap me with bread and call me a sandwich, my feelings are way to deep.

I saw it coming, kind of. I didn't expect him to actually do it, but in the back of my mind I knew he might try. My father was waiting outside my sibling's school, fortunately for me, he hasn't been to their class in three years or in the school so he doesn't know where anything is.

He didn't look much better from when I left him, he gained a bit of weight, has grown a beard. He looked terrible honestly.

I was halfway out the car, frozen slightly. Getting a grip, I turned to hunter, "Hunt, could you get the kids today?" I asked pleadingly, he nodded looking slightly confused but didn't ask questions as he unbuckled his seatbelt. "Bring them straight to the car." I muttered getting out the parked car, closing the door behind me.

"What's wrong?" Jaxon asked walking towards me, I didn't even notice he had gotten out the car. Not answering him I walked towards my father, my mind going haywire. Jaxon seemed to figure out what was happening when a string of swear words came out of his mouth.

"Anthony" I said gulping down the lump in my throat, as he jumped his head snapping towards me. "You shouldn't be here" I said, my voice low and emotionless, what I was going for, now I just have to keep it up.

"Son, I need speak to you, I didn't know where else to go or how to reach you" My father said, using 'son' once again, I raised an eyebrow. "You have five minutes. Talk" I snapped, surprising my self at how cold I was sounding, my father obviously shocked too.

"I'm almost losing the house" he said, I would feel sorry for him but he reeked of beer and his breath smelt of smoke, another thing he started and is wasting money. "Stop waisting money on beer and drugs." I said simply, shrugging. Annoyance flickered In his broken eyes, obviously wasn't the sympathetic response he was looking for.

"Gabriel, son. I need you, losing your mother it broke me and with out you and the kids there, it's like I lost you as well, I can't lose the house too" he said pleadingly, my blood was starting to boil, seeing where this guilt trip was heading. "I just need a little bit of money, to pull through" he had the audacity to ask, I stared at him with complete disbelief. Is he serious right now?

"What makes you think I have money? I'm living off nothing but generosity of my friends. I have nothing. Even if I had a spare dollar, your dreaming if you think I'll give it to you! After all you did, you're not getting a cent from me" I growled angrily, I'm now embarrassed to be related to this man.

"You stole three thousand dollars from me!" He yelled the remorseful act disappearing, into the angry, selfish man he has become. "Yeah and it went to paying for your wife's funeral, that you couldn't be arsed to go too" i retorted, glaring at the man in front of me. Jaxon stepped beside me, his body slightly blocking mine from the disappointment in front of me. That shut him up.

I shook my head, mentally disowning my father. "I'm not your son. Jack and Lilly aren't your kids. You lost that right the minute you laid a hand on me. If I see you anywhere near them, i will call the cops." I growled out turning away from him, Jaxon following close behind.

"Thank fuck for that i don't want a faggot for a son anyway, and since I have no kids anymore I sure as fuck don't have to pay school fees. Funeral? I was to busy fucking a wh-" Anthony didn't get to finish his sentence, since Jaxon's fist met his jaw, I looked back, tears stinging my eyes

"You're pathetic piece of shit!" Jaxon roared his fingers around his next, "i fucking hope you lose the house and if you dare go near him I will tear you up limb from fucking limb. Mark my words" Jaxon spat venomously, I've never seen him so angry before. Hunter passed me grabbing Jaxon and pulling him away from the pathetic human being.

I felt my heart break and my world start to crumble once again. What now?

Chapter ~12

M oments ||Gabriel Lewis

Tears, I was sick of the little salty water droplets that stained my cheek. I swear I'm going become dehydrated with the rate I'm going.

Jaxon has his arms wrapped around me once again, holding me together as he whispered not the worry, everything will be fine. I'm not believing it at the moment, I have ten cents to my name, and I have to provide over a grand of school fees for the twins and well me, but that's optional.

How can someone throw there lives away, push away everyone and change completely change over the span of a month, just over. It completely blew my mind. I'm the one that's suppose to spiral out of control and become dark and depressed not him.

"What have I done wrong? Why does life start to look up and then tear me down. Can't I get a break?" I said wiping my tears, laying back in Jaxon's bed, relaxing slightly on the comfortable mattress. Jaxon mirroring my action his arm laying on my stomach. No my heart is not getting any ideas, not at all.

"You've done Nothing wrong. You've gone above and beyond with keeping your siblings safe and happy." Jaxon said softly, my mind was really trying its hardest, but it had a hard time with Jaxon's fingers that were grazing bare skin, was proving a hard distraction to ignore.

This boy is killing me. Killing me softly, not with his song but with affection.

"What am I going to? I can't keep scabbing off you. I don't know where to start for a job, if I do I probably have to drop out if I want to earn enough money to support the twins with school, and pay back you for all you've done." I rambled nervously, the thought of the bill that I owe Jaxon makes my head spin.

"Gabriel, listen to me." He said pulling his self up on his arms which were now on both sides of my head. Not helping my case at all. "First. Get this stupid idea out of your head that I would ever accept your money. Cause I won't, so stop worrying about paying me back my money, it's not going to happen, i have enough money. " he said his beautiful brown eyes staring into my soul.

"Second. Your job, is to take care of the twins, and if you want something to do then clean the apartment." He said his head leaning down slightly. I went to argue his deal as it wasn't fair. Before I could, Jaxon's lips were on mine.

Holy fuck.

His lips were soft as he kissed my frozen body. My brain was having a hard time telling my heart to keep beating. My lips thankfully became responsive, kissing him back with the no experience that I had. Sad life I know.

"I'll worry about the money" he whispered, his brown eyes staring down at me, a small smile on his lips. "You worry about what you're going to wear for our date" he said, making my eyes bulge slightly. Date? Jaxon Coles doesn't do dates. "Don't look so shocked" he said laughing pressing a kiss to my forehead before laying on his side.

"You're gay?" I blurted out seeming to find my voice, he chuckled his arm wrapping around my waist, pulling me into chest. "No. I'm demi-sexual, I think that's what it's called. I'm attracted to your personality, or as google says, the emotional bond between us." He explained his fingers intertwining with mine.

"Gabe?" A small voice mumbled, turning my head back I found my brother, stratcat cuddled into his chest. Hair sticking up in all directions. "I can't sleep" he mumbled, I smiled softly opening my arms for him, he waddled over climbing on the couch, curling up on my lap.

We were watching a random documentary series, about famous bridges around the world. This episode was about the Sydney harbour bridge, Jaxon had an arm around my shoulders, Hunter sitting in one of the chairs with Tara on his lap sleeping.

"What's wrong bud?" I asked softly, knowing that something was on his mind if he couldn't sleep. "Is daddy angry at us?" He asked looking up with tired eyes. I sighed softly tightening my grip on him. "He's not angry at you sweetheart. Me and Dad don't agree on a few things" I sort of told the truth, he wasn't angry at the twins, he is just a drunken scum.

"Does he still love us?" He asked, my heart was going out to the boy. I feel sorry for the twins, they don't hardly know what's going on. "Jack, daddy is a bit confused at the moment. Okay? Deep inside he loves us." I said softly pressing my lips to his forehead. "But no mater what, I will always love you alright bud?" That's something I can say confidently and honestly.

After a few minutes Jack's breathing evened out. Pressing a kiss on top of his head, I rearranged my grip on him, before standing up. Walking to our room, placing him into bed with his sister.

"You know, The government pays for fostered children's education" Jaxon said when the ending credits rolled of the program. I turned to him, with a raised eyebrow. What was he suggesting?

"My parents will take you all in, with out a second thought. You turn eighteen this year, after your birthday you can become a legal guardian of your siblings if that's what you want. You can still live here or stay my parents estate" he offered, still watching the tv. I gasped at him, I can't ask that of him and his family.

He has already done so much, I can't ask him to foster us as well. Though I don't know particularly if what we are doing at the moment is legal. My father is unstable and unfit to take care of children, the house is definitely not a place to raise children healthily.

Fostering would take stress off my shoulders with school fees, but what about everything else. As much as Jaxon tells me not to worry about paying him back, I have to. This isn't a few dollars here and there, this is thousands of dollars that he has spent on us. That's not something I can forget about or just sweep under the table.

"just think about it, the offers there if you want it" Jaxon said softly slapping my leg as he got up from the couch.

"Are your together yet?" Hunter asked casually, making me choke on thin air, it's a skill trust me. He laughed "I ain't blind my friend. I see the loved up expression between you two. Contrary to popular belief, Jaxon Coles is a complete romantic sweetheart" hunter said his fingers running up and down Tara's arm.

I small smile made it's way to my face at the thought of Jaxon stressing as he sets up some romantic date. "Whipped and definitely together" hunters voice brought me out of my thoughts, he was smirking widely, I rolled my eyes at him. "We kissed, that's it" I mutter a blush coming to my cheeks, thoughts of this afternoons activities coming to mind.

"Well I'm happy for you my man, you deserve some happiness. Oh and best friend hunter is here and ready to punch either one of you two if you hurt each other" he said, narrowing his eyes at the end of his sentence making me laugh.

I could handle Hunter being my best friend, he's a good guy that makes me laugh, his been nothing but kind and welcoming since I met him. I already got the feeling that he would have my back no matter what.

Claire is someone I guess I would class as a friend, she has been kind to me ever since I've met her, i apologised for what I said to her before my mother died which she waved off saying I was right.

I've also gotten to know Tara a little, she is absolutely lovely, couldn't hurt a fly. She tamed Hunter's wild playful side, which was nice cause him and Jack together can be a tiring. "Thanks Hunt" I said giving him a nod, which he returned, before standing up with Tara in his arms. "I'm going to take sleeping beauty to bed. Night Gabe, jax" Hunter said walking away.

Jaxon came and sat by me once more, his arm automatically wrapping around my shoulders. "It's good thing I don't feel like getting punched by hunter anytime soon isn't it?" Jaxon said, I laughed nodded and agreeing.

"Is that talk of experience?" I asked raising an eyebrow, he chuckled nodding. "Yep, we were going through a rough patch two years ago, I said and did a few things I shouldn't of and bam, right hook to the jaw, Fracturing it." He explained rubbing his jaw.

"A trade off between a packet of sour skittles and a Xbox game. Best buds again after that. "

Chapter ~ 13

- -

Work || Gabriel Lewis

Cleaning, not the most fun job there is in the world but it was something. The hours were not the greatest either but they worked for me, plus I got a nice pay check for it. I finally found a job as a cleaner at a hotel, all I needed to do was clean dishes, do laundry and sometimes clean a room. The hours were from 9pm till 1am, again not ideal but it's something.

Jaxon wasn't particularly impressed since I would be walking to and from. That was a huge benefit with living at Jaxon's, he was more in the town centre so everything was walking distance. The hotel was a ten minute walk from the apartment so it wasn't that far.

"Here. If your walking the streets in the middle of the night. You need one" Jaxon said handing me a white paper bag, the apple logo on the side of it. My eyes widened looking inside, seeing a box of a new iPhone. "Mine and Hunter's numbers are already in there, as well as Tara and my mother's since she bought it. I would of put Claire's in for you but I don't have her number." He rambled lightly.

Picking up the box I opened it to reveal the white and gold phone, pressing the button at the bottom of the screen, making it light up, a picture I never knew was taken, of me and the twins set in the background. Placing the bag down on the table beside me, I wrapped my arms around Jaxon's neck, he laughed wrapping his arms around my waist returning the hug. "You know I'll pay you back, I've got a job now" I muttered determined.

Leaning back, his hand came to grip my chin, pressing his lips to mine for a second time which put my heart in cardiac arrest . A guy like him should wear a warning, cause it's dangerous and I'm falling.

"You don't have to pay me back. You being happy and mine is enough" I'm starting to seriously doubt why people were scared of him, Jaxon is a huge softy and a sap. Nonetheless I will pay him back, if he likes it or not.

"That was puke worthy, honestly. Soon you'll be shitting rainbows" Hunter's voice came from behind me, making me laugh, turning slightly to face him. "That was nothing compared to what I had to deal with, Rocket man" Jaxon replied. I laughed at the reddening cheeks of Hunter.

"I gotta go, I don't want to be late for my third shift" I said being ballsy and pecking his cheek before slipping out of his grip, grabbing my phone. "Oh here, it's old but does the trick for now" Hunter said handing me a faded red cover for my phone, I grinned thanking him as he put it on.

"Hello Gabriel" my manger greeted, as I walked through the doors, into the warmth, allowing my body to defrost, I really need to get some better winter clothes. At least a good jacket to keep out the icy winds.

"The kitchen needs a hand till its closed, could you run a vacuum through the halls, it's silent so it won't disturb anyone. There are two rooms that need to be cleaned out up on floor 3 and 7. After that just the laundry need to be ready for tomorrow morning. Thanks" Harold said giving me a run down of my jobs I need to do today.

I nodded heading through to the staff room to place my things in a locker before heading to the kitchen, placing the bright yellow rubber gloves on and starting with the dishes that seemed to be piled up. "Oh thank god your here, we've been understaffed and busy." One of the kitchen staff said patting my shoulder.

It was all industrial and automatic so my job as dishes boy wasn't that hard, load a tray with as much as you could, place it in, pull the lid down and dry things from the last run, repeat. Easy.

The vacuuming was easy too and took me a few minutes on each floor, I ended up doing the rooms while I was on the respective floors. The laundry wasn't hard either, just putting sheets and towels in large washing machines and dryers and pressing start, by the time the cycles Finnish I would almost be done folding the last.

This job is very much repetition, doing time consuming or boring little jobs that no one else wants to do, which for now I couldn't care cause at the end of the week I'll have earned some money, hopefully enough to buy the weekly takeaway Chinese order on Saturdays. Hopefully.

Our schedules worked perfectly, Jaxon and hunter left for the gym at around 4pm and came back around 6:30, we would all have dinner, the kids would go to bed around 7:30, I would leave at a quarter to nine for work. Come back around one am, go to bed then wake up for school six hours later. I worked every night apart from Monday's and Friday's, since Jaxon and Hunter had to 'work'.

I'm not 100% comfortable knowing where Jaxon's money comes from. The thought of Jaxon getting hurt didn't sit well in my stomach, but Jaxon seems to enjoy it and be good at it. Who am I to stop him, he gets damn good money from it too, more then I do, that's for sure.

Progressively over the past month that I've been working, the number of nights I'm with Jaxon has increased dramatically. By the end of the month I'm more or less sleeping full time in Jaxon's room. My clothes have migrated to a space in his large walk in robe.

Monday's and Friday afternoons we visit mum's grave, the kids talk all about what's been happening, telling her all about the imaginary adventures they go on with Hunter. Jack has commented on my relationship with Jaxon making me blush and laugh.

Tuesday's have been dubbed date night, the night me and Jaxon go out to do something together.

Saturday's we usually did something together with the twins, if that was going out for a meal or catching a movie. Most of the time Hunter would tag along with Tara and on rare occasion Holly or even Claire would come. We had it once where everyone tagged along , so we went to minigolf. It was fun.

School was actually fun for me, which I'd never thought possible, the rest of the school is slowly by surely accepting me as a normal human being, I even get hello's thrown at me in the halls, again never thought possible.

"M-morning Gabriel" a voice called out, to the side of me, I smiled greeting the girl back, though I had no idea who she was, curly red hair, freckles and glasses, I feel like if you were to time in red head nerd tumblr photos in google she would pop up.

The people who greeted me weren't so much the jocks and cheerleaders, they were still trying to get over the fact that I became friends with the kings of the school. The people who greeted me were lower down the popularity food chain, which was kinda cool, I guess I'm not as intimidating to talk to, unlike my two bulky body guards, who honestly aren't that scary.

I mean, they addended my little sister tea party over the weekend, with the dolls and toys that she has been given generously by Jaxon's family and Tara. Sadly for Jack, his sidekick (Hunter) and stratcat was roped into the tea party too, so his fight against the imaginary pirates had to be delayed. The troubles of being a 5 year old.

For all that wanted to know, they won the fight against the bad pirates with lightsabers and saved damsel in distress, princess Lilly from walking the plank into the lava sea.

You could say next instalment of Pirates of the Caribbean, is going to be interesting.

"Well aren't you Mr. Popular" Hunter muttered poking my shoulder playfully. "Yeah the nerd rebellion is starting, watch your selves" I replied walking into the mathematic class which I had with both of them. They both laughed.

Jaxon's hand held mine under the desk, his thumb drawing circles, Hunter was behind us with no one sitting next to him so no one could see out interlocked hands.

We haven't come out or made our relationship public, cause it's no ones business and neither one of us what to deal with the backlash. Jaxon had told his parents about our relationship a few weeks ago, which also meant he came out as Demi-Sexual. Which honestly was interesting for me to know what Demi-sexual really is.

Holly was excited and happy pulling me into a hug, and begun planing our wedding. She mentioned that I was already family and Jaxon's offer for them to foster me and the twins still stand.

The money I've earned from work has allowed me to pay my own and the twins school fees, I've figured out it takes me two whole pay checks to pay the monthly fee for us all. I divide the amount over four pay checks. I made

Jaxon a deal that I would pay the schooling and I wouldn't push to pay back the amount I owed him before. I wasn't a hundred percent happy but i wouldn't get it any better, if he had it his way he would pay for everything.

For once in my life I'm actually happy.

Chapter ~ 14

G ifts || Gabriel Lewis

Birthdays. The last time I had a party, was when I was seven, I invited my whole class, two of which were my friends. I decided I wanted to have my birthday at Mac Donald's. Every kid's dream party I'd say, out of the twenty four kids i so kindly invited. Six came, which I guess Is an alright turn out since I was the quiet kid at the back of the class that no one knew.

The twins never really had a party for their birthdays, not at home anyway. I'd usually bake cupcakes for them to bring to class but that's about it. We celebrated their birthdays in the hospital with Mum, if it happened to land on a Sunday, Dad would join giving them a few dollars each as a present. I always tired to get them a small gift.

My birthday was just over a week after, I never really celebrated it after the money got tight and Mum got sick. Mum would mention it to me quietly giving me a kiss, but that's as big as it got.

This year how ever, the twins will be getting spoilt. Holly just about had a fit when I told her about our lack of birthday party's and gifts over the years, she vowed to change that and has planed a birthday party for the twins.

I'm proud to say that I could afford a gift for both of them with money to spare. This probably would be the best give I've ever afforded.

Today was the day , Monday, April 2nd. The twins birthday. Last night we baked chocolate chip cupcakes with purple and green icing for the classmates.

Holly has been busy with the apartment all day, while we were in school. Picking the twins up, they came racing out with large grins on their faces, hugging them tightly to my chest. "Gabe where's your glasses?" Lilly asked glancing at my face.

Jaxon wanted to see if contacts would work which they did so I've ditched the glasses for contact lenses and holy macaroni, I look different with out glasses, the people at school thought so too with their jaws scraping the floors.

"I'm wearing invisible glasses" I whisper as if it was a secret, she gasped her eyes growing comically wide. Jack began his tirade of questions about the invisible glasses making me laugh.

When we entered the apartment, I jumped slightly startled as a small group of people yelled surprise. Gifts bags and wrapped boxes covered the dining table; Enough snacks and treats on the kitchen table to feed an army; colourful streamers and balloons decorating the apartment.

The twins looked around with wide eyes, their mouths agape with shock. "Happy birthday Lilly and Jack" Jaxon said ruffing up Jack's hair. The two looked at each other, large grins spreading on their faces before they squealed loudly jumping about, engulfing us in hugs, yelling thank you's loudly.

"Don't thank us kiddos, this was Fairy godmother Holly's doing" Hunter said laughing as he picked Lilly up, earning a kiss on the cheek.

Jaxon's and Hunter's parents were here along with Tara and a few older kids that I guessed were foster children of Holly and Kane. I thanked Holly numerous of times for what she has done.

"Honey like I said, a friend of Jaxon is a child of mine, those kids mean the world to Jaxon. They are absolutely beautiful children that I can't help but adore, So it's my pleasure dear."She said pulling me into a hug.

When present time came around, the twins were completely spoiled rotten. They got clothing, toys. Jaxon giving Lilly a cook book while Hunter proved the custom made 'Lilly's kitchen' apron and oven mitts. Jack got nurf and water guns from Hunter while Jaxon gave Star Wars merchandise.

I got up quickly to grab my gifts, two identical looking boxes. Handing it to them, I was slightly nervous, I knew they would love it but I didn't want to upset them.

When they opened it, it was two bears, dressed in my mother's favourite dress. Mummy writing in orange cursive writing since that was her favourite colour on the left foot, the day she died on the right.

A few weeks ago me and Jaxon had gone to the house when we knew Anthony was out. The house was a rubbish dump to put it nicely, and smelt like one too. Beer cans, cigarettes and take away food containers littered the house, the sink was filled with dirty dishes which have been there for a long time since the food on it was rotting.

We grabbed the rest of our belongings which he made easy since every thing was in a pile in the corner of the rooms, and I grabbed the Home tapes of when I grew up and of the twins. On a particular tape she was saying good night to them, so I recorded it.

"Press the hand" I muttered,

'Jack, my precious prince, have sweet dreams and know that mummy loves you'

'Lillian my beautiful princess, have sweet dreams and know that mummy loves you'

Tears welled up in their blue eyes, as they hugged the bears tightly. I smiled softly wrapping my arms around both of them "now you have a little bit of mum where ever you go"

As with any relationship, there are disagreements and fights. It's to be expected really, and that's what was happening now. Jaxon was getting defensive and over reacting about something, apparently my half hearted apologies weren't good enough. I groaned falling back on the bed, Jaxon still ranted on.

It started over me questioning if I should get my own place, Not that I i want to get away from Jaxon it's just, I sometimes feel like a burden, the twins have their days where they are just little pains, and I feel bad that hunter and Jaxon have to witness it, along with a list of other things. Jaxon didn't agree.

"Jax just forget that I said anything okay?" I mumbled putting my shoes on, noticing it was almost time for me to leave for work. He sighed walking up to me, his hand cupping my cheeks, making my head tilt upwards. Leaning down and pressing his lips to mine, why is he so damn addictive? It's not fair.

Before the make out session became something more, I stoped it. I smiled up at him my fingers curling around his hands, "I need to go to work" I mumbled, three words almost slipped out, but got stuck on the tip of my tongue. The words honestly surprised me that they surfaced or got so far.

Tilting my head I pressed a kiss on the palm of his hand. The words Itching to come out, as if the moment was perfect for it, but I bit my tongue and stood up. Moment effectively ruined.

A knock at the door, allowing my mind to shut up the heart and concentrate on other things then me being in love with Jaxon. The door opened softly to show Lilly and Jack, I raised an eyebrow at them wondering why they were still up. "Are you guys fighting?" Lilly asked quietly.

I smiled softly, opening my arms inviting them in, they bodies ran up to the bed, Jaxon grabbing Lilly around her waist and picking her up, Jack climbing on to the bed and curling up by my side. "We aren't fighting sweetheart, I just don't agree with your brother on something." Jaxon said softly, sitting down placing her on his lap.

"It's nothing to worry your pretty little minds about" I added pressing a kiss to Jack's head. "We will worry. You and Dad don't agree on stuff, we never see him anymore" jack pointed out, his eyes narrowed, lips turned into a pout, which was his serious face, well adorable to others.

"That's different Jack. Dad has gotten into some bad things which make him a bad person. Someone who I don't want you around cause it isn't safe. Jaxon and I, we are fine, we just have different opinions which sometimes clash. Nothing to worry about bud" I explained as good as I can.

"Jaxon isn't scary like daddy was and he didn't hurt gabe" Lilly commented making me smile in agreement. "I'm not scary?! We'll see about that" he joked his fingers assisting her stomach making her burst into a fit of giggles. "Am I scary now?"

I love how my six year old siblings aren't intimidated by Jaxon or hunter in the slightest yet, school is terrified.

Jaxon said he would take care of the kids so I could go to work, pressing kisses to the three children, one of which getting a special kiss as Lilly says.

I bid goodbyes to Hunter on my way out, my phone in my pocket. The wet streets were almost deserted, since no one wanted to be in the rain or cold. Even though winter is over, the nights can still be freezing.

"Hey faggot" a voice came from behind me, before I was pushed to the ground. Is this really going to happen? Are they serious?I cried out as a hand gripped my hair harshly, Jame's ugly face came into view.

"Your not so special now with out your pathetic friends to protect you" he laughed, I heard of her people laugh as well so he wasn't alone. God dammit why me? Why now?

"Get up" James growled, pulling me up by my hair, ouch that hurt. Two of his apes held my arms so I couldn't protect my face, as his fist came flying. After a few punches they dropped me, and started with their feet. Pain erupted from all places around my body, I could feel blood pouring from my nose. I was almost happy when everything turned numb and faded into nothingness.

Chapter ~15

P rovoked || Jaxon Coles

"There are scouts coming to tomorrow's fight" Hunter said as I sat down on the couch, the twins were sleeping peacefully, finally. Both asked a few more questions about their dad, that I had to dig up quick lies up, following Gabriel's stories.

Their father was a prick of a man, I can't understand how someone could completely ruin their life when they have young kids that need them. I know that Gabe is amazing in that respect cause he has raised the twins for the past few years. It's not fair on Gabe, he had to grow up quickly to make sure his siblings were taken care of, and when he needed some one his father wasn't there. I was.

"Scouts? For what?" I asked, playing a game on my iPad. I know Daniel mentioned that I should go professional with fighting, but I never thought I was good enough, I'm just a school kid trying to make some money on the side. Plus professional means I would have to reveal what I've been doing to my parents.

"For the big leagues my man! You do what you do, win. You might get a contract, get some big bucks , make a name for your self!" Hunter said excitedly waving his hands around to make a point.

"If you get a contract you can get proper training with a professional trainer, things I can't help you with bro." He added watching my reaction. "Let's first see if they show up and if by chance their interested then I'll think about it" I responded, groaning when my phone went off, huffing I got up, jogging across the room to find my phone. Eyes furrowing at the unknown number.

"Mr Coles?" A male voice came from the the other side, sounding slightly annoyed, "yes, speaking?"

"I'm Harold Witiker, manger of Honey Pot hotel. You are put down as an emergency number to call for Gabriel Lewis correct?" Harold asked, my concern levels skyrockete.

"Yes. What happened? If he okay?" I rambled out, already searching for my car Keys "well nothing happened that's the problem. He never arrived for his shift. We are currently understaffed and need him today." Harold said which did nothing for my concern levels. Never made it? He left an hour ago!

"He left an hour ago! Fuck" I snapped hanging up the phone, Hunter was already at the door, keys in hand. "Let's go" hunter said opening the door.

The twins.

"I'll go. Stay here, if he comes back, we can't leave the twins alone." I ordered, he nodded throwing me his keys hesitantly, I nodded to him as I walked out the door. "Be careful" he shouted down the halls.

My eyes searched the the side walks as I drove the route he would of walked. Through there was no luck, I couldn't see him anywhere. Picking up my phone i called him, but it never went through, like his phone was off, which he never did.

My heart was quickly becoming heavy with stress and concern. I drove to the only other place I could think of that he would go. His fathers.

Walking up the overgrown path, I wondered how gabe and the twins live in this shit hole, the last time I came I got to see inside and the living conditions were horrible. Gabe didn't have glass in his window for fuck sake. Pounding my fist on the door, I heard grumbling and a sting of curse words. I didnt really care, if that son of a bitch misplace a hair on Gabe's body I will kill him.

"What the fuck do you want?" The disgraced of a man snapped as the door swung open, I almost gagged at the rotten smell. "Where's Gabriel?" I asked narrowing my eyes at him, pathetic man.

"Some bitch called earlier about him but fuck if I care about the faggot. I told her to fucking keep him" Anthony slurred.

I'm trying so hard not bash this man up, "where is he?" I growled my hand gripping the scruff of his shirt, "tell me before I dig your grave using your head as a shovel" I threatened, fuck his breath stinks. How Gabriel came from this piece of crap will always be a mystery.

"You're fucking him aren't ya? He turned you into a faggot" he rambled, I growled pulling him out side before slamming him into the wall. "Where is he?" I asked once again.

"Where his fucking mother was, and hopefully end up next to where she is" the scum mumbled out. Once punch to the face was enough to knock the thing out. Pulling him back into the house I slammed the door and walked away.

Hospital. Fuck.

Breaking a few speed laws, I arrived at the hospital in record time. Racing into the reception area. "Gabriel Lewis? Where is he? What happened to him?" I asked the front desk lady, who looked startled, but checked the computer anyway, well I hope she is checking for me.

"My I ask your relation to Mr Lewis?" The lady asked, her voice soft and almost calming as if I wasn't freaking out. "Jaxon Coles, I'm his boyfriend and only family who gives a damn" I answered, she gave me a small smile nodding,

"Gabriel Lewis, found badly hurt in front of Gilly's bakery. He is in emergency surgery now." The lady, Sarah said. Somebody hurt him and I have a pretty damn fucking good idea who it is. I'm going to kill the assholes.

"Seeing as Gabriel is under the age of legal maturity and the response we got from his father, it's our duty of care to inform child services." Sarah said, my heart dropped.

Fuck.

"Susan, is our child service representative who has been put on the case. Am I right to assume you know of Gabriel's situation?" She asked softly, I nodded. "Okay, this is the card for Susan, she will be here tomorrow. Now I advise you to go home for tonight, as Gabriel won't be able to see anyone until tomorrow." Sarah said her voice calm and kind which honestly is the only reason I'm not ripping the walls apart.

"Gabriel has siblings correct?" Sarah asked, I nodded, "Jack and Lillian. But they don't live with their scumbag father. They live with me, so does Gabe. They have done since their mother died in February" I explained, Sarah nodded typing it in. "Okay, if you leave your phone number, I'll give you a call if anything changes okay?" She said, I nodded writing down my number, thanking her before walking out the hospital.

"Where is Gabe?" Jack asked as we got in the car, Hunter got in the other side after helping Lilly in.

The minute I got home last night, I called my mother out of bed and told her and Hunter who listened in what happened. Hunter was pissed just like me. Mum said she would meet us at the hospital. Which is where we were headed.

Arriving at the hospital, we got the kids out, they maybe young but they figured out that their brother wasn't well. Mum and Dad were already, waiting for us. She pulled me into a hug before fussing over Lilly and Jack.

We were ushered into a office, hunter took the kids out for breakfast to keep them occupied. Susan introduced her self before she started asking questions about Gabe and the twins lives. we answered what we knew about his past, and told them what happened with their mother and asswipe father.

She told us the process of what will happen, apparently Gabes birthday is next week, much to my shock, he never told me when is birthday was. So technically he was an adult and allowed to legally be his own guardian, as for the twins being so young will have to go into foster care if Gabriel isn't financially stable enough to support his twins.

Mother mentioned about their past with fostering kids which probably helped us a lot with getting the custody over the twins, as it would be for their best interests to be close to their brother and be with people they already know and trust.

Karin, who is Mum and dad's agent concerning the foster kids that are put in their care was called and gave a reference of sorts for Mum and Dad and sold the deal basically.

Gabriel's father will be arrested on charges of neglect, two counts of abuse and a few other charges that were outstanding. This all happened over a meeting that lasted over three hours.

All I need now is food and Gabriel. The later being more important. Mum and Dad will handle all the paper work for the twins. Since Gabe is so close to being eighteen, there is no point putting him through the foster system.

Shaking hands and thanking Susan who honestly was extremely kind and helpful. I walked to the front desk asking for Gabe. I was slightly nervous to see him, cause I honestly didn't know the damage, I mean he had to go into surgery so it's not going to be pretty.

my heart shattered and my blood boiled at the sight of Gabriel. I don't even walk in, I turned and walked out of the hospital. Determined to give the asshole who did this a bit of his own medicine. Just worse.

Chapter ~ 16

C hange || Gabriel Lewis

My body numb yet I could feel somebody gripping my hand, I could feel somebody rake their fingers softly through my hair but my body still felt numb.

My head felt weird and fuzzy, I could feel something up my nose which felt weird when I breathed. It was weird cause as much as I tried to move or wake up from this weird limo of consciousness i couldn't.

I don't know how much time goes between me being half conscience and not, I could hear voices though they sounded like echoes you'd hear deep in a cave with some body at the entrance shouting or it was muffled like somebody talking through a wall. Some words were loud and others I could barely hear.

"Gabe. Miss. Up. I. You" was all I managed to compute along with some-body gripping my hand, it made no sense to me, before i could try and think about what it all meant I was swept up by nothingness again.

When I came back there was no voices just a constant beeping and I couldn't feel anything nor the person that held my hand. I assumed the everyone left. My mind wasn't as weird anymore, like the fog cleared, allowing me to have normal thoughts and hear things normally. I felt tried, even though I've been asleep for this whole time, which must of been a large period of time considering no one was here anymore.

Considering I've been hearing the same beep for the last three years with my mother, I know I'm in hospital, why still is a mystery. My last memory was Jaxon and Hunter coming home from the gym. After that it gets dark and non understandable, the mess of sound and blurred pictures hurt my head, drained my energy trying to remember it.

It was made clear to me that I spaced out since the last time because people were around, I could finally recognise the voices as my head wasn't messed up and my hearing was back to working properly.

"We gotta tell him slowly, a lot that has happened, it will be big thing to process" I recognised as Holly's voice. How long have I been out for? What has happened?

"The question is, what do we tell him first? He has been through so much. I feel sorry for him man. Poor guy hasn't had a rest" that was Hunter, Sounds like I'm going to have fun when my body decides to come back to the world of the living.

When my eyelids decided to seperate, I was alone, I think. My vision was blurry from not having glasses or contacts in. I noticed my body feeling a lot heavier then usual, my limbs felt like 10 kilo weights were hanging off them.

Moving my stiff neck was one of the most satisfying moves I have done, it cracked the whole time, loosening the knots in my neck. I saw a set of glasses on the table beside me, I sighed in relief moving my arm which was a challenge in it self. Once my world got a little clearer, I found the light switch. Bad idea. I was blind once more by the sudden harsh, bright light. Once my eyes adjusted, I saw cards and drawings piled on the side table.

Glancing down I saw my arms that were littered with a few nicely made bruises. For a minute I was highly confused on why, but soon memories of what happened flooded my mind.I'm surprised he went this far, the effort and time he put into making my life hell, it's honestly sad. He needs to find a hobby, what doesn't include bashing my face in.

"Mr Lewis, glad to see your awake." A nurse said softly as she walked in, "I'm sarah, do you know why your here?" She asked picking up the clipboard off the foot of my bed and checking things.

"Yeah I was beat up, pretty bad I guess" I muttered once again glancing at my arms. She nodded "you had a large blow to your back right side which damaged your kindy quiet severely, you had to have emergency surgery as your kidney, which was essentially leaking poison through your body."

Well I damned, James and his band of apes did some damage. I almost feel sorry for what Jaxon will no doubt do if he find out or he has already figured it out. "The other injuries you've sustained were minor, the internal and external bruising which will heal over time" Sarah said,completing the task she had to do while telling me why I don't feel anything before bidding good byes.

For some reason I was exhausted after that small exchange, so I didn't fight the tidal wave of darkness that consumed me.

I was woken by the door opening and voices muttering to each other. "You know some people are trying to sleep here?" I croaked out jokingly blinking to get my eyes readjusted to the the bright lights.

"Gabe!" The voices of my siblings yelled, before I was attacked gently in hugs and tears. "We missed you gabe" Lilly whispered in my ear, I smiled softly managing to wrap an arms around both of them. "I missed you too guys, have you been good?" I replied receiving innocent looks and quick nods. Chuckling they continued to tell me what I missed, Im gathering I've been out for about three days, and missed quiet a bit.

"Hey bro, how you feeling?" Hunter gripping my wrist softly, pushing my fingers down to make a fist before first bumping it. I rolled my eyes letting out a chuckle at his antics.

"Better now, where's Jaxon?" I asked glancing around the room, Hunter tugged at the collar of his shirt, letting out a nervous laugh. "He is uh he is locked up for the next two weeks" Hunter muttered biting his bottom lips. My jaw dropped, what hell happened? I close my eyes for three days and bam Jaxon gets arrested.

"Let's just say James has a broken nose and a few bruises. Him along with half the football team have been either expelled or suspended and James has joined Jax behind bars but for a little longer." Hunter explained, sitting on one of the seats that were provided, my jaw was slack in shock.

Jumping Jesus on a pogo stick.

Well as much as Jaxon behind jail doesn't sit well in my stomach, I'm sorta happy that James and others have been dealt with, should teach them not to pick on people.

"When do I get out?" I asked groaning as a sharp pain shot up from my side, I guess I'm not sitting up then. "If the doctor's happy you should be out Thursday, the 12th" Hunter answered messing with his phone. What a lovely birthday gift? I get to get out of this sanitary box.

"Holly will be over in half an hour, she has a bit to explain to you. A lot has happened in the past few days, my man." He said picking Lilly up and placing her on his lap.

"Did you take care of the twins by yourself the past few days?" I asked curious. "No, Tara stayed over, Holly was around everyday and my mother even came by" Hunter explained shrugging as if it wasn't a big deal. It still amazes me that I've got such an amazing new support system that is so willing to help me.

I enjoyed talking to Hunter, he told me about his little brother who died when he was young, that's why he connects with Jack so much. Jack fills a bit of the hole that the death of his brother made. Lilly was just a bonus for Hunter, I've noticed that he has gotten closer to Lilly the past few weeks.

"You are like family man. Not only to Jaxon, but to me too man." Hunter said flashing meA grin, laughing when Lilly gave him a hug "you're my family too!" Lilly said her voice muffled by his chest, Jack voiced his agreement. Hunter grinned widely, hugging Lilly back.

Holy came in a few minutes later, immediately fussing over me, like my mother would if I scraped my knee. "my child!" She kept repeating, pressing her lips to my forehead. I smiled, a warm feeling filling my chest.

"Now dear, a lot has happened because of you being here. as a hospital, they have a certain duty of care when it comes to children not having a safe home life. When you were identified, the hospital called your father who responded in a negative way, which raised concern that this was the doing of your father.

Jaxon managed to talk to the hospital staff and clear a few things up with your living arrangement. But, your father isn't safe or stable enough for children to be around, therefore it's state law that the children are taken away and the parent is dealt with.

Because the twins are so young, the living arrangement wouldn't of suffused, since non of you boys are of legal age yet. I know you were hesitant about the fostering offer but unfortunately its out of your hands in this situation. I've spoken with the child service representative at the hospital and we are now in the process of getting state custody over the twins. Who will end up in our family's care, as fostered children.

There was little point putting you through the foster system as you are turning nineteen in a few days. So you'll stay in hospital until your birthday, after that you are of legal maturity, you're considered an adult. The twins will legally have to live with me, but visits both ways are limitless.

As for your father, he has been put arrested and put behind bars. For neglect, child abuse and other crimes he has been found guilty of."

Well pin my tail and call me a donkey.

Chapter ~ 17

Love || Gabriel Lewis

Home is where the heart is, that's what they say and it's partly true. Unfortunately my heart is behind bars at the moment serving 2 weeks for bashing James up, but the injuries were no where near as bad as mine.

My father has landed himself 7 years in jail, for the charges against him. Apparently he stuck his foot into some drug ring, which was how he survived financially for the past few months, delivering drugs to people, he even got a (stolen)car.

Opening the door, my eyes widened at the group of people who were there. "Happy Birthday Babe" Jaxon said making my head spin slightly in confusion, I thought he was locked up?

"Okay so maybe i bent the truth slightly. Maybe it was only one week instead of two and he might of gotten out yesterday." Hunter said as he walked passed a smirk plastered on his face. I rolled my eyes and laughed lightly since my ribs were bruised, laughing can be quiet painful at the moment.

The twins ran past me and engulfed Jaxon in a hug, commenting on his absences. Laughing he picked them both up, pressing kisses to their cheeks. "hey kiddos" he greeted placing themon the ground once again. Satisfied with the greeting they wondered off, Jaxon's eyes following them with a small smile, shaking his head his beautiful eyes finally looked up at me.

I smiled, I always thought Jaxon would be a good father, he is amazing with the twins and children, I love watching his soft side come out. Walking, well limping slightly towards the perfect looking boy. "Happy birthday babe" he said softly his arms wrapping around my waist, his lips pressing to mine, I smile wrapping my arms around his neck.

It wasn't a surprise when Hunter ruined the moment, telling us to get a room. Honestly sounds like an awesome idea but not today.

The small party was fun, though I was drowsy from the medication that I was on, but I enjoyed talking to everyone. My eyes widened when they started giving me gifts, i never expected people to remember my birthday let alone give me gifts.

The gifts were thankfully small, so I didn't feel overly awkward accepting them. The twins decorated a mug with 'best brother' written on it, one half was Lilly's design and the other Jack's.

I wasn't expecting Holly and Kane to give me anything considering their family has already done so much for me. I couldn't possible accept a gift, but I was forced into accepting the new iPhone, since my last one, was smashed beyond repair from the attack.

Hunter handed me a wrapped box, I glanced in side, my cheeks growing warm as i closed the box I glared at Hunter half heartedly, he laughed loudly.

Tara gave me a box filled with salts, candles, bathbombs and soaps, since it was her family business in making them. The twins already putting dibs on the bathbombs they wanted which I knew will be used for them anyway.

Claire handed me a beautiful drawing, which brought tears to my eyes. It was a drawing of my mother before she got sick. It was of a photo that Jaxon sent through to her. I gave her a hug thanking her multiple times. Claire is quiet the artist.

Jaxon just smiled at me, pressing a kiss to my cheek. I thanked everyone once more as people started to leave. The twins said their goodbyes since they were sleeping at Holly and Kane's Home. It felt weird not having them around, not saying goodnight or tucking them in.

They had to stay at Holly and Kane until the paper work is finalised, after that we can make some sort of plan to spilt their time being with me and with them.

"I'm sorry to hear that Gabriel" Harold, my manager said genuinely, his mouth pulled into a straight line. I've missed almost three weeks of work with out any explanation, so as you can figure I lost my job. Today is the first day that Jaxon allowed me to take a step out side the apartment, I figured I better beg for my job back.

"The attackers are locked up for a bit and a restraining order against them so they won't be bothering me anymore" I said shifting my weight to the other foot.

"Gabriel you were a great worker but unfortunately in your absence we have hired another. I wish I would have known of your situation sooner, I wouldn't of put somebody else on." Harold said an apologetic look falling over his older features.

I sighed, in the back of my mind I knew I had a fifty fifty chance at getting my job back. Having the twins schooling being paid for was definitely a stress reliever for me. Now I only had to worry about paying for my own education.

Jaxon, as always had told me not to worry about it, that he will take care of it, which until I get another job, he will have his wish. Bidding goodbye to my old manager, I walked out the hotel where Jaxon was waiting for me.

I haven't been able to leave Jaxon's sight, unless I'm with someone, which can get annoying sometimes but I don't complain cause I like feeling that I'm worth something to someone.

My feeling for the supposed 'badboy' of the school is almost scary how much I adore and love him. He has very quickly stolen my heart and held it captive in his brown eyes. The words are always at the tip of my tongue when we fall asleep or a moment reveals it self, but i always hold my tongue.

I'm terrified that I've fallen way to fast and he didn't feel the same, I don't know if I could handle it not being said back to me, though I know he feels something for me.

Classes have started their preparation for exams, I can't believe my time in school is almost finished and to be in the place I am in at the moment is completely mind blowing. So much has happened since February, I sometimes can't believe the events that's taken place, shaping my future.

I've applied in the medical field at a few local colleges, i would like to become a doctor but I know that's a long stretch so a nurse would satisfy.

"You alright babe?" Jaxon asked pulling me out of my thoughts, I turned smiling at him. "Yeah, Im good" I replied gripping his hand as he drove us to the shops so we could pick a few things up before we headed home.

It burned. My skin was on fire and my heart was burning a hole through my chest. Are the Jonas brothers having a reunion? cause I'm burning up.

A moan escaped my lips, causing the temperature in my cheeks to rise, as Jaxon's lips assaulted my neck, leaving marks that I'm sure I'll be having to hide for school tomorrow.

My fingers gripped the hem of his shirt tugging it upwards softly. That article of clothing was in the way of my viewing pleasure, i grinned when the shirt came off, my fingers trailing the defined ridges of his god like body. My eyes studying the tattoos for a few seconds, my breath was caught in my throat at how beautiful the man in front of me truely was.

"My self control is struggling" Jaxon growled, making my pants a little tighter, at his hormone filled voice. My lips curved into asmile, wanting nothing more then his self control to take a hike. He was breathing heavily, arms shaking slightly where he boxed me in.

"Fuck me already." The words tumbled out of my mouth like a avalanche. Jaxon's jaw dropped slightly at my beautiful display of the French language, his eyes coming to meet mine, darkening with lust and desire, though he didn't move.

"As much as I would greatly enjoy fucking your delectable ass into next week. I'm not going to" Jaxon muttered, making my heart drop into my stomach. I really fought hard not to let the cold sharp blades of rejection and insecurities cut through my confidence and heart but my fight was useless.

"Oh" was all my body managed to come up with, my eyes casting downwards since I didn't want him to see the slight hurt his answer gave me even though I could understand.

"Babe" Jaxon whispered his fingers gripping my chin and tilting my head upwards to face him. "Your ass is mine tonight, don't worry your pretty little mind about that" he whispered, pressing his lips to mine softly, "Losing your virginity should be something special." he muttered, his lips trailing down the side of my neck as his arms wrapped around my waist pulling me closer to his body.

"Everything's special if i get to share it with you" I replied my arms wrapping around his neck, my spout of hurt is quickly being forgotten. I felt his lips curve into a smile, his fingers tugging my shirt over my head before guiding me to the bed.

His body was hovering over mine, eyes sparkling. "I love you Gabriel Lewis. I'm fucking in love with you completely and now I'm going to show you how much" Jaxon confessed staring down at me with such emotion.

My heart just about exploded, as I gaped slightly at him. Tears built up in my eyes but I kept them at bay, linking my arm around his neck, my fingers gripping his hair, pulling his lips towards mine.

"I love you too Jaxon Coles."

Chapter ~ 18

Epilogue || Gabriel Lewis

Life is pretty weird if you think about it, I mean who knows what tomorrow brings? Who knows where you will be in 20 years. I certainly didn't expect my life to be what it is now.

I have two children for god sake! I know I basically raised the twins but still I have two humans that call me Dad! How bloody weird!

My baby boy, Xavier. He was our first child, I fell in love with him the minute I set eyes on him in the state foster home, his story almost mirroring my own just at a younger age. His mother died in a car crash and his father became abusive. He was small and terrified of the world around him, so my heart just went out to the boy and I needed him to be mine.

Then there is Autumn. She is my little spit fire, her personality matches her fiery red hair, and blazing green eyes. She is definitely Jaxon's child, same short temper, same determination that her father has, with the soft loving side that has strong protective streak to protect the people she cares for.

Jack and Lillian just celebrated their twenty fifth birthdays, they have grown into to beautiful young adults, with their own family's to take care of. I'm an uncle of a nephew and two twin nieces, who are absolutely gorgeous and I adore.

Jack married his high school sweetheart, Isabella and welcomed my nephew Kole into the world two years ago. Jack and Hunter have become successful business owners. Co-owning a sporting franchise together, Iron Productions which specialises in creating sporting equipment, they have a few Gyms being opened around the America too.

Lillian is engaged to Mark, a man she met on a pilgrimage through Cambodia four years ago. He works as a priest in a private all boys school. Lilly works as a special needs teacher assistant in her local school. They welcomed twin little girls Cassandra and Talia, 7 months ago. My nieces are absolutely beautiful having their mother's blue eyes and their fathers curly brown locks.

Hunter is in the process of Migrating to Australia, so Iron Productions can become an international brand, plus Australia is one of the country's that has expressed interest in the company. He married Tara a few years ago and are expecting their own in 6 months, the gender has been kept under wraps.

Jaxon Coles has become a big name in the MMA fighting industry, having won championships left, right and centre, breaking stereotypes as he goes. Amazingly there is only one other male fighter that is openly apart of the lgbtq community.

His fighting career has slowed down slightly in the past 5 years so he could be with his children. He has opened up his own gym and training school for young wanna be fighters. The gym is heavily sponsored by jack and hunter who provided all the equipment for it.

I've some how managed to get my self a masters degree in nursing which has led to me being chief nurse at the local hospital. Though it's stressful and has long hours I love my job.

"Dad I'm going to become the president of America" Autumn said walking out of her room, hair brush in hand. "And when I am president I'm going to put all the stupid people in jail" she said determinedly. I chuckled pulling a brush through her red, curly locks, humming in response.

"What happened to being a formula one race driver?" I asked my eight year old daughter, smiling amused at her, shrugging she looked at her purple painted nails "that was so yesterday Dad, I'm a big girl now, I need to have a proper job when I grow up" she stated, making me laugh as I thread her hair through the thick hair band before pressing a kiss to her cheek.

"Princess you can do what ever you want, as long as you're happy darling" I said as we walked out her bathroom, her small hand gripping mine.

"Papa! Stop!" My son squealed between his laughter, I chuckled at my husband who had our son trapped in his arm while his free hand tickled a red faced Xavier.

"Papa! I'm going to be next president of America so that means I'm the boss of the house" Autumn stated, which paused Jaxon's tickle attack, distracting him enough for my ten year old son to escape and run towards me.

"Is that so? Little miss" Jaxon asked eyes glowing with amusement, straightening up and crossing his arms over his chest, raising an eyebrow. Our daughter nodded mirroring his actions, not intimidated by her father in the slightest.

"Yes Papa that is so. And I order you to.." She said biting her lip glancing around the room, before pointing to the door "my first order as boss of the house is for papa to get my shoes" she said.

I chuckled wrapping an arm around Xavier's shoulders as he leaned into me. I watched as Jaxon walked slowly forward letting his arms fall to his side, Autumn stepped back ready to bolt if needed, but she was to slow, getting engulfed my Jaxon's large figure, laughter and squealed were muffled by his chest.

"Come on you two, let's go we are already late as usual" I stated grabbing the car keys and the backpack that stored the kids gadgets and other thing. Jaxon turned to smile at me, autumn laying his arms, cradled to his chest, giggling, red hair sticking out in all places. I should of known her hair wouldn't stay neat for very long.

Jaxon has always been Autumn's hero, she was a Papa's girl completely, though she looks up to him and completely adores him. She will push to see how far she can take things, questioning his authority and even his opinion on things. She was a clever little girl who has Jaxon wrapped around her little pinky.

Both of them have but for different reasons. Xavier has always been the more quiet and reserved persona, he has come so far from what we got him just over 4 years go, he still likes to retreat into his shell but also knows how to get what he wants from Jaxon.

Today we were going to the Lillian's homestead to visit the little ones, since she lives just three towns over, it takes just over an two hours drive to get to her place in the country. We see each other regularly but not as much as Jack since he lives 10 minutes away.

Every month we have all have lunch together at someone's house, Holy and Kane had it last month, this month is Lilly, next is Jack, then ours and occasionally we will do a meet up at Hunter's.

We were surprisingly the first to arrive, which never happened before since we usually the last people. The kids ran up to the house, their two golden retrievers meeting them half way. Rosa-Bell and Butch, the two friendliest dogs you'll ever meet, both are obsessed with children.

Grabbing the things out the car, we walked up, laughing at the two dogs that surrounded us, their tail wagging. Walking into the house, I smiled smelling Lillian's famous apple pie.

"It that apple pie I smell, Lilly I love you" Jaxon said walking into the kitchen, I laughed following behind. "It's why I made it" Lilly laughed wrapping her arms around Jaxon, "Aunty! I'm going to be president!" Autumn said walking in, I chuckled giving my sister a hug, pressing a kiss to her cheek.

"President? What happened to being an astronaut?" Lilly asked turning her attention to her niece. Me and Jaxon laughed at that faze that was a few weeks ago, she was completely set on becoming an astronaut for Nasa.

"I grew up Aunty, I'm also afraid of heights and the stars are in the sky! That a long way up! What if I fall? Being President i won't have to worry about falling off any stars" she stated as if it was the most obvious answer, Lilly laughed nodding her head in agreement.

Jaxon gripped my hand pulling me out the kitchen to the living where Xavier was talking to Mark. "Hey Mark" I greeted smiling holding out my free hand for him to shake. "Hey Guys, how was the drive?" He asked letting my hand go to shake Jaxon.

With in an hour everyone had shown up, I was sitting on the couch with one of my niece's in my arms, Jaxon's had his arm around me as he watched the baby in my arms, his fingers gently brushing over the brown curly tuffs of hair.

Autumn was on the floor in front of me, playing with Kole, the giggling two year old who was just starting to talk. Xavier was taking to Jack, a grin on his face as he laughed at what ever Jack told him.

I could be more happy of the close knit family I have, I'm proud knowing that I can financially support my self and that my siblings tho they had a tough start they are happy and successful in their own lives.

It's moments likes theses what i cherish the most, everyone was happy and together. My kids have a large support system, growing up in a life they deserve, even if their starts might of been tough too.

"What are you thinking?" Jaxon asked softly bribing me out of my thoughts, I turned slightly, smiling at him.

"My life is perfect and none of this would be reality if it wasn't for you. Mr Badboy of the school and now Husband" I said chuckling, he smiled softly.

"And your my Nerd"